I0727022

Saints of Mary's Projects

Saints of Mary's Projects

Alex Avila

Ape Press LLC
California • New York

An Ape Press Book
Published by APE Press LLC
Saints of Mary's Projects Copyright © 2021 by Alex Avila.

This book is a work of fiction. Names, characters, businesses, organizations, places, events and incidents either are the product of the author's imagination or are used fictitiously. Any resemblance to actual persons, living or dead, events, or locales is entirely coincidental.

APE Press LLC
P.O. BOX 2051 • San Bernardino • CA • 92406

Author Alex Avila
Book and Cover design by Alex Avila
Photography and Graphic Art Design by Alex Avila

www.avilaproduction.com

Library of Congress Control Number: 2021915742

ISBN: 978-1-7377057-0-3

APE Press LLC: 2021

10 9 8 7 6 5 4 3 2 1

APE Press
California * New York

Here are some of the Community Organizations I support and Work With:

www.smcc-ke.com (Supporting Families and children raising funds for a resource center; clinic, orphanage, and classrooms)

www.thebeep.org (Building affordable housing for people of color)

www.youthactionproject.org (training and creating jobs for youth)

www.yvyla-ie.org (youth leadership academy)

www.timeforchangefoundation.org (affordable housing, and innovative entrepreneurship center)

www.nationalblackgrad.org (improving Black graduation, retention, and enrollment)

www.justsb.org (building a human centered economy: The People's Plan)

Table of Contents

Acknowledgment

Thank you, Juan Delgado and Kathryn Ervin, for your patience, guidance, and commitment through this entire process. You both helped me see the light – it has been an honor. I like to give mad shouts out to the entire St. Mary's Housing Project in the Bronx. Rest in Peace Scott, love you, bro. Big shout out to moms and pops for forcing me to read a dictionary throughout elementary school. Mad love to Mia Avila for holding me down throughout the years, David J. Kalke, a.k.a my other dad, for instilling principles and values I practice 'til this day, the entire Avila - Clotter – Mcdowell –Ragsdale – Stone – Ruff – Arzu – Middletons – Buffong – Williams – Browns and Carter family. Yo Kenwood, Butter A.K.A Joseph Ruff A.k.A. B-Suave, Q, J.J. and the McDowell family, Blue, Titi - Stacey - Rich, Mrr. Red, Tone, Suga J, Jimbo, Melissa, Al Uno, BX Tim, Ray, Cuzzo George, Tio Frank, Tio Nofi, Crazy Cynthia, Fly Guy, Big G, Stan, and all of my blood relatives out in the world. Big shout out to the Garifuna community and all of Central America. Shout out to Pernal Walker and Victor from the All Saints Lutheran family, the Bronx. A mad Big Ups to Rickerby Hinds and the Hinds family, Kerb a big thank you for allowing me to learn with you on your glorious journey. To all the SCIPP families and friends, The Fellas, Black Scholars Matter, CHICCCAA, All Saints Lutheran, LCM, 4e, Central City Luther Mission originals. The Fam living in Iowa City – Rob, Sara, Valarie, and anyone I couldn't fit on this list. Much respect to Dottie for getting me the hook-up, Andrew in the English department, Diane Podolski, and President Morales. Dr. Lewis King, Jean Kayano, Kevin Cosney, Miriam Nieto, Rosemary, and the family with all respects. I want to thank Daniel Walker, Ed Gomez, Lenard Lopez, Jean Delgado, and Mark Henry. Michelle Bracken, Rosie Alonso, Chance Castro, Michael Cooper, Elisha Holt, Orlinda Pacheco, Tristan Acker, Lawrence Eby, KL Straight, Daiana Rodriguez, Nikki Harlin, Tim Hatch, Allyson Jeffredo, Cindy Cotter, James Brown, and Bolin Jue. Respects to Sunny for wearing ten different hats and helping us through graduate school. St. Mary's, we did it.

Dedication

Forward

Juan Delgado
Professor of English, Former Poet Laureate
Former Provost of CSUSB
Author of several award winning books
Dara Weir: Contemporary Poetry, Awardee
American Book Award, Awardee

Avila is a talented interdisciplinary artist who gracefully fuses photography, poetry, performance, and video. He vividly presents portraits of St. Mary and its people, providing us a vision of a place that extends beyond its geographic markers and boundaries. Avila dramatizes a community that goes across cultures and generations, a community of conflict because of its social and economic inequalities, its crime, and violence. Yet, St. Mary is not solely a community of divergence and difference but a community of shared experiences and values.

Through his art, Avila gives us the opportunity to witness a community of solidarity, celebrating its graffiti, its public singing, and daily encounters. St. Mary is democratic because of its multiplicity of voices, its ruptures of individual expressions, and its intersections that link its people. It is a community of continuity and change, and Avila from poem to poem affirms what we know is true: A life is better lived in the company of others, striving together for the common good.

Forward

Kathryn Ervin
Professor of Theatre Arts, Theartre Director
California Educational Theatre Association, member
Kennedy Center American College Theatre Festival Outstanding Awardee
Black Theatre Network Lifetime Membership Awardee
NAACP Pioneer Awardee, inducted into the College of Fellows of the American Theatre

This book is a window and a mirror. It will give you a glimpse into the world of Saint Mary's Project and you may see yourself. This is the work of Alex Avila. I met Alex at the California State University, San Bernardino. And I met him again at a community center and again, as a performer with Project 21 Dance company. I am proud to have served on his MFA committee.

Alex is an artist activist whose work in the Inland Empire has reached out for people of all ages and encouraged them to tell their stories in film, theatre, and in pictures, dance and poetry. This collection includes stories of some people who are gone and introduces some who are emerging. Here you will find people and places to make you laugh and remember and think. See? Alex is an artist activist and this book is a work to make you think and move.

Enjoy

Introduction

Saints of Mary's project is a multifarious literary work recounting a city's historical, personal, social, political, and cultural constructs birthed by violence. This trilogy follows my journey from growing up in St. Mary's projects to my introduction to organizing at All Saints Lutheran and moving a grassroots culture into cities, academia, and politics.

The majority of the pieces in this book are part of a live and digital performance. These multifarious literary platforms include theatre, museum displays with live poetry, spoken word, short films, and poetry videos. I coined the terms Multifarious Presentation, Multifarious Literary Performance, and Multifarious Prose in 2015. The idea was to capture the innumerable devices we use to convey messages—the personification of St. Mary's begged for diversity in disseminating her story, our stories. In the Bronx, St. Mary's Housing project is the foundation where most of this literary work occurs.

The modern-day Griot (storyteller) is a Poet, guiding his audience through the social inequalities and disparities that plague St. Mary's community. The Poet shares traumatic personal insights while simultaneously utilizing writing as a form of survival to the conditions of the Bronx. This multifarious literary work highlights the metaphorical and physical cycle of violence and survival. One of these survival tools is utilizing the pen over the gun, and the Poet becomes the living testament to this method.

I phonetically exploit sound to introduce my audience to Hip Hop, Salsa, Blues, Dowap, Jazz, Reggae, and funk. Some of these phonetic explorations allow for the recreation of percussion instruments such as the drum. The repetitive words or phrases are part of the African tradition to engage the audience in a call and response. The tension between melodically fun tones and dramatic text creates complexities for these entities to exist in the same space. Thus the performance of St. Mary's is a rollercoaster ride of emotions and deep thoughts. If you are interested in a live performance or want to connect, email me at alex.avila4e@gmail.com with the subject matter stating, "I read your book, St. Mary's."

WELCOME TO
St. Mary's Park
Houses
Property of
New York City
Housing Authority
NEW YORK CITY
HOUSING
AUTHORITY

Rent

Rent 4 life

Over 2,000 people
lived on my block
I only knew three
people who went to
COLLEGE

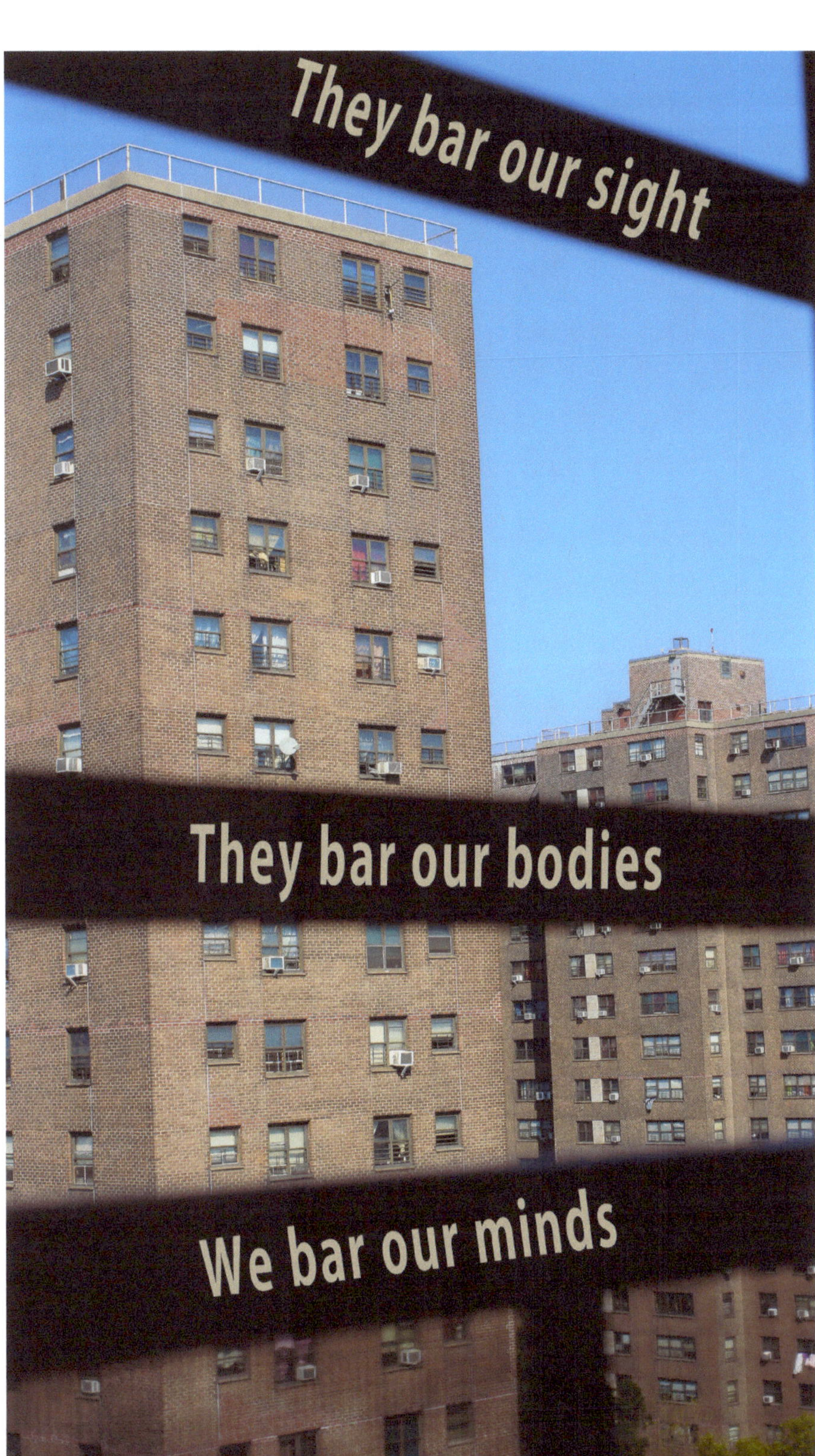

They bar our sight
They bar our bodies
We bar our minds

BETTER LATE THAN NEVER.
BELATED HAPPY BIRTHDAY!
We hope you had a wonderful celebration!
The Bronx's Birthday 163?
R.I.P Lenape People

Mad Questions aka MQ

MQ:
Yo fam
you don't think
it's bugged out
how we sitting here
in St. Mary's

Jonas Bronck
who founded the Bronx

murdered the natives
Lenape people
to build his estate
he named St. Mary's?

now here we are.

PINCH:
Yo, I'mma get me a slice pizza
you need
you
anything
from the corner?
It's too early for all that.

The Break

Two hairpins
wrestle with one another
under the crescent moon.
Kack –kack

June's eye ping pong
long chattering cabby busy streets.
Kack – kack

Flix's fingers
move pins
like chopsticks
hunger
itching for another hit.
Kack – kack

June
like usual
bugging
his boy
in the middle of making love
and a doorknob.
Yo Flix, hurry up, man.

with Bobbi pins

Mixing his Spanglish with old action films
Flix turns his cracked dried lips
Cabron, you can't handle the truth. I'm the shhh.

Kack
Click
the sound of metal aligning
as one drum.

June and Flix both nod
and turn the knob.
for the next vic' to get rob.

Witch Doctor

My fourth grade teacher
Ms. Madera says
If anyone you know is sick
call 911 you can
save their lives
In my apartment
'buela coughs hard
curled up on my bed like a baby
'buela tough as cement
this was my first time seeing her
stretched out on my bed unable to get up
She just got home from work
and my first words were
Mami — Mami 'buela sick call 911
'buela the babysitter discipliner
family gatherer spiritual leader
migrant worker
who doesn't understand the word No
in Spanish or English
Mami rushes to the bedroom
places her winter hands on her forward
she withdraws her hands as if she touched a fire pit
Mami — Mami call 911
I cried
from my bedroom door in my Batman pajamas
'buela says No in a weakened voice followed by a curse
 Gringos con sus medicinas
Spitting flem into an iron pot
She motions Mami to come closer
and whispers into her ear
Mami runs to the kitchen and rips

the leaves from the plants on the windowsill
the Bronx lightens up whenever its snows
the night is not as intimidating
Mami tienes que llamar 911 'beula's really sick
She ignores me as if in a trans
She turns the kitchen into a science lab
Boiling water
in a rusty iron pot
adding herbs
ripping more leaves off the plants
She pours the hot mix into a coffee mug
grabs a big metal spoon
I follow her every move
from the kitchen to my bedroom
Mami tells 'beula
Aqui lo tengo está caliente teng' cuidado
Mami blows on the spoon
As she raises 'buela's head to drink
I wake up to the smell of banana pancakes
Sun rays breaking into our living room
Fresh coffee made from scratch
Eggs dancing in a frying pan
I remove the bundles of blankets off me on the couch
A seventy year old lady is working our kitchen
with the energy of a teenager
she tells me
dale prisa y ponga su ropa
vamos al parque de St. Mary's
I stare at 'buela in shock
'buela laughs and says
Gringos con su medicinas
Wiping the sleep from my eyes I return the laugh saying
Yeah, Gringos and their medicine

Broken English Revisited

Con permiso Señor, me puede 'ayudar fix my English.
It seems I have broken it... como un espejo caído.
Shattered across the nation with my
arroz y frijoles and a bit of sazon.
Con razon my tongue speaks with flavor.
Por favor excuse phonetically my behavior,
for I add the /e/ before the /s/ sound producing
eschool- espace - espoon - esky.

eSorry for espeaking with pasion y amor.
As our mother's sing in their kitchen reciting bachata Senior,
Tengo un Corazón
(boom boom)
motivado de esperanza y de razón
(pea-ning- ning- ning- ning ning).
Tienes un tape so that I can wrap it around my broken English?
I can krazy glue it, so my Spanglish doesn't go spilling out like my
cup of Sangria.
I need to fix it so that I can graduate and get a job dice mi tia Maria,
because everybody doesn't eat fried platanos with the grilled red
green peppers,
and onions on the side.
My Aztec, Arawak, and Taino pride needs to find a place to hide.
I gotta water down my African blood that rages like the falling river
inside.

If I could speak like them Señor, I can fake the funk and my dark
skin can get by.
En el nombre del padre, y en sus espíritu .
As I blow out my Virgin Mary candle Senior,
I pray that you can help me fix this problema
because I also overheard the other students in class say,
 Real Americans don't speak broken English!

Once Upon a Bronx

Rananchqua
The Bronx
home to Lenape
whose blood color the soil brown
rich iron fed
trees greened
 Fall
Red
Brown
Yellow
 Leaves
Jonas Bronck
peace sully
musket -fi re-volleys
Matrilocal
Divided
like the Aquahung River
Red black Mesingw's face
Tear
Drop
Small pox
put potato colored
skin in pine box
Turtle Wolfe Turkey
met by the Fire Drills
In the middle of St. Mary's
race crying wind
break across brick buildings
There you can hear the
Lenape people
if you
stand

Still

barbecue spareribs

just the way
Adam   loves it
You can see him
under the apple tree licking
his fingertips

her onion white eye

Deep Pan African fried
candy yam skin
America tried

to Jezebel
you
stuck to
your guts
like chitterlings
ling   ling   ling
rang liberty bell

blood pressure pot roast
golden   black brown
her   children
hung   down
the Persian tree
swung in the
open winter breeze

Eve's Soul Food

s l o w burn
turn @ 180° sbattered hair
don't care cooked stares
salted cured pain with sweet potato smiles
labored seven times a 100 back aches
to feed her sweet peas
just to make collard

greens

her kettle screams into Martin's dream
integrated white rice and beans til this day they
still steam

never tire to cry
while in the kitchen
cutting a slice of
cinnamon crusted apple pie

HOUSING AUTHORITY

In Loving Memory
GOYO
Mama
7/21/76
6/16/95
PEDRO

Gata Lady p1

hair moved past her chewed off ear
like the ocean
to cover sounds of morning
like seashells
rush hour honking horns
crowded sardined subways
packed like beans in buses
a black cat fuses
with twenty meows

a frail
body rises
from a squeaky
full-size mattress

fingers rub grey eyes
to sky-lit
bright blue
over brown buildings
under
scattered waves of clouds

Fila long-haired cat
with three legs
rubs her body
against Gata Lady's
feet   which
lands
on chilled faded
black tiles
cat eye slippers   bring
warmth to spider-webbed
vein foot
as they slide into fluffy
hello kitty slippers

Boy's Legos   Build St. Mary's   Brick by block
building blocks   minds   scaffold dreams   with pencils
sketch an emergency   exit   prop door open
with Crayola box   vomit words off rooftops
let letters fall on winter   spring forward
burning ideas
like the secret to staying young
is building words on a page
so that his   inner childhood
can remain unharmed
on a stage
built by
    Legos

FAILURE'S
MY BEST FRIEND,
COMPANION ON
MY EVERYDAY
JOURNEY.

SUCCESS IS AN
ASSOCIATE
WHO VISITS
OCCASIONALLY.

WE SHALL OVER
COME
OVER
WE SHALL OVER
WE SHALL OVER
we shall over
we shall over

Love someone
something
anything

Start with
YOU.

Wounded Knee

Running savagely
towards him
eyes boiling blood
cottonmouth

behind the barrel
of his gun
Jonas Bronck waits
patiently
for the wild running

fingers squeeze
blast echoes trees

a Lenape falls
to his . . .

Too Easy

Don't beat yourself up especially when your opposition wants to destroy you. you'll make it ...

21 to Zip

Tevin spins
off left pivet
turns like faucet
arms
stretch
shoot
drops in the bucket
like water
splashes of dreams
drip salty sweat
Nothing But Net,
   Check!
Screams the teen
sun baked acne
redden the
yellow skin tone
Yo-yo-yo-yo Tone,
You gotta run that back b'
Dribbles black ribbed leather
between rundown dusty sneakers
On my word Tone
I'mah be the best player ouch' here
n' I'mah take my Nana ouch' dis joint
you feel me.
Tone focused on Tevin's hip
confused
crossed over
Tevin leans in with shoulder
finger rolls
Nothing But Net,
   Check!

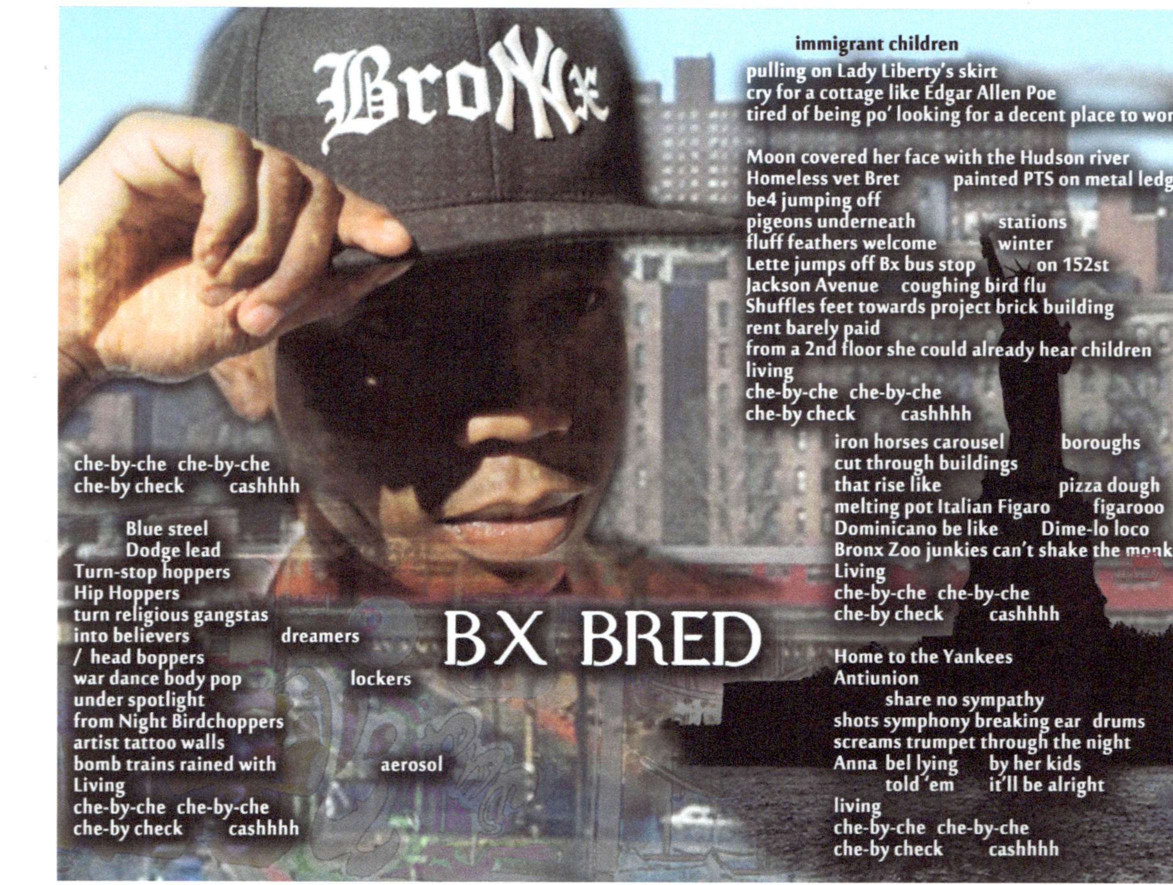

Bronx

BX BRED

immigrant children
pulling on Lady Liberty's skirt
cry for a cottage like Edgar Allen Poe
tired of being po' looking for a decent place to work

Moon covered her face with the Hudson river
Homeless vet Bret   painted PTS on metal ledge
be4 jumping off
pigeons underneath   stations
fluff feathers welcome   winter
Lette jumps off Bx bus stop   on 152st
Jackson Avenue   coughing bird flu
Shuffles feet towards project brick building
rent barely paid
from a 2nd floor she could already hear children
living
che-by-che che-by-che
che-by check   cashhhh

iron horses carousel   boroughs
cut through buildings
that rise like   pizza dough
melting pot Italian Figaro   figarooo
Dominicano be like   Dime-lo loco
Bronx Zoo junkies can't shake the monkey
Living
che-by-che che-by-che
che-by check   cashhhh

che-by-che che-by-che
che-by check   cashhhh

Blue steel
Dodge lead
Turn-stop hoppers
Hip Hoppers
turn religious gangstas
into believers   dreamers
/ head boppers
war dance body pop   lockers
under spotlight
from Night Birdchoppers
artist tattoo walls
bomb trains rained with   aerosol
Living
che-by-che che-by-che
che-by check   cashhhh

Home to the Yankees
Antiunion
          share no sympathy
shots symphony breaking ear drums
screams trumpet through the night
Anna bel lying   by her kids
            told 'em   it'll be alright
living
che-by-che che-by-che
che-by check   cashhhh

Tracks

Rubber around limb
fingers slap skin
tap-tap-tap
Nothing
Come on – come on – come on

Bronx High's
prom king
A track star
who could've modeled
for ancient Greek Olympics
make Zeus proud
how the crowd
would scream
Go – Go – Go Smitty Smacks Go

A name coined
after his opponent was lapped
he slapped
his own back
as his cleats
kicked dust
like horses   on a betting track

Come on – come on – come on

Hands jiggle needle
shake
Eyebrows levee sweat
break
He can't find a good track
Eyes closed to feel skin

bulge
Wood boarded windows
fights morning sun from
trespassing
fingers passing
over dried   pus   skin
Come on – come on – come on

Now drags   his feet underneath
the shadow of train tracks
that drips
with iron   piss   spit
looking
for a new blue line
on his worn-out tracks
hiding in   a burnt
out   building
a block from St. Mary's
ignores a rat
sipping Coca-Cola
from a white wrinkle bag
of recyclable bottles
tap-tap-tap
Nothing

Kicks off   New Balance kicks
they look like
worn-out flip flops
souls callused
right hand
massage's left naked foot
spread gap between

the hallux and long toe
metal breaks skin
injects medicine
he   breathes   slow
lays back flat on a barbequed floor
rubs stomach
a cracked mouth drools
eyes open sounds a silent chant
go   go   Smitty Smacks   go

Bugged Out

It's green butt
lit my index finger.

      Parece como un roach.
 I said, sitting still.
      It's a lightning bug
      they visit St. Mary's every summer.
         Craig said, smoking his stick picking his afro.

The green paint chipped off
the long wooden benches.
KRS ONE is blasting from the eighth floor.
The small playground filled with kids laughing
chasing one another.

Older folk reflect upon the day
against a yellow moon.

Craig and I are chilling.

      Mi cumpleaños está cerca, I'm almost eight.
      He chuckles, padding his fro. I push my nose
      closer to my finger, its wing is stretching.
      The day they stop visiting Lil' Man, you know
      St. Mary's is in trouble.

I looked at Craig perplexed vexed thinking;
where would the bugs go, and why would St. Mary's
be in trouble.

Sassy's Summer

Sassy Sandy
Spitting Sunflower
Seed
Summer sweat
Slushy smooth
Slim
Skin
Shimmering
Against
St. Mary's

Funky Joe

Funky Joe
stunk
with Bourbon blues
down
Jackson Avenue
My baby baby Betty Bo oooooo
Jazz dripped
from his shiny wet lips
Babbbbbbby Betty
Baby baby baby Betty
Tongue swing swung
Sung
Right
Left
B -Bop down bodega shop
Dowop dowop
dowop dowop
baby Betty
on his back
rags worn out
with time
You can see
Funky Joe
Blow
warm air into
his fist
limped bruised waist
from sleeping
in train tunnels
He hip ha ha ha hop
pass 154st   just a couple blocks
from St. Mary's

Body rock base
Baby Betty
2 am
Monday morning
from 2nd floor
Lette's ex-husband yells
          Yo Funky Joe
                    Can you please shut the hell up
I'm trying to sleep
A whisper is heard
coming from the Hub
On 3rd
Baby   betty
what   did
I do
to
loose
youuuuuuuuuuu

Ghetto PTSD

An argument ensued
Two men
Two am

    Where's my money

One hand
Grabs
Bottle
Breaks
Bottle

    No . . . No . . . HELP . . . SOMEbody

Two hands
pushed
Begged

Bottle breaks hands
Bottle breaks face
Bottle breaks skin
        chest
        stomach
        back
        tongue

legs   he can't
he won't   run

No one
comes to his rescue

We all listen
pretend not to see

I still carry that man's screams
bottled in my dreams

Freddy Flip Time

What time is it?
Freddy Flip Time...

He sold watches by 3rd ave
on 149th street.

I got your Rolex
Rolex- Rolex
that'll make your wrist Bowflex
and get any Mamacita to stop on the drop of a dime
to ask you for the time.

I got that Movado
to add to your bravado.
Como no...

Un flaco,
su piel was a bit blanco.
A Boricua
who wore a du-rag on his head
trying to discipline his natural curls to wave
like the Atlantic ocean,
or better yet, like those black kids from Morehouse's projects.

What time is it?
Freddy Flip Time...

Puerto Rican flag tattooed across his chest
Black Panther fist on his right arm.

Watches – come get your watches.
They'll make your kids look cool
going to school
I got everything from Mickey Mouse, Batman, and even that Wolver-
ine fool.
Como no…

He kept a fresh a haircut.
His lineup was straighter than a #2 train
going from the Bronx into the tunnels of Manhattan.
You found Freddy Flip
Uptown   Downtown   all over town
with his baggy blue jeans
New York Knick's jersey
and a Yankee fitted ball cap
carrying a black briefcase.

His watches never worked past two weeks
but peep
he made you feel good in the few moments he hollered at you in the
streets.

What time is it?
Freddy Flip Time..

Pero coño   Mamacita   ven pa'ca
Did your man forget to call you beautiful today?
Let me help put that frown away.
I gotta watch for you worn by Queen Elizabeth herself
pero you're much   much   more gorgeous
 de verdad.
I lay this on your wrist, and with your chemistry, it's like a time bomb,

she smiles.
The men will drop dead when it goes off boooomb!
I caught two heart attacks standing next to now.
Como no…

In the gummy floored subways, he called college kids looking for
work "Mr. Wall Street."
He told the shy heavy-set girls on the bus stops
how their dimples were deep enough to plant a seed and watch a
flower grow.
Tourist buy watches from him because he made them feel right at
home
He never sold cops or judges any of that fake stuff because they
were sensitive, you know.
No kids or family.

When Freddy Flip died
hundreds came with their watches
and when the Wall Street exec raised his watch at the funeral and
asked the crowd
What time is it?
They all responded
Freddy Flip . . .

DJ What brought us together the crowd sang dance
to words sounds
that serenaded the children of St. Mary's

DJ What

Brown Babies in Cages

A toddler's fingers
pushes a ladybug
underneath metal doors
towards freedom

Go free
whispers a four-year-old
while pushing a ladybug
underneath metal doors

Go free
and go find Mami
Mami should be coming soon

Her fingernails cracked
packed with dirt
from Honduras   Mexico
New York   California

Her fingernails cracked
packed with her mother's
perfume the smell of Jasmines
Disneyland
Jasmine
Jasmine
that's what her mother named her
Jasmine's 4
locked up behind metal doors

Brown babies in cages x2
Brown babies

Jasmine's 4
pushing a ladybug underneath metal doors
A room full of babies
coughing
A room full of babies
crying
A room full of babies
with diapers that haven't been changed in days
A room full of babies
who won't eat
A room full of babies
with bedsores from sleeping on concrete

What's more, concrete than
Brown babies in cages

This is us
Welcome to the US

Chilling with the SUN

His heart
melts
like
Cocitos
on a summer Sunday

Whenever she
glances over her shoulder
Smiles

    Chavo:
    Yo Ajax just ask shortie out already?

    Ajax:
    Chill sun. . . chill sun, it ain't like that B'

    Ajax:
    Then what's it like?

Dreamer Revisited

Strawberry foot blisters burst.
Hard potato hands reach towards them to nurse
A North American dream quenches her thirst
with humane labor, a small apartment, and future grandchildren
going off to college
They will have no knowledge of;
slaving 10 hour days, no breaks, smothering heat, glazed with
sweat backs beaten with stress, having ten mouths to feed with 10
cents to stretch.

A thousand yards from the US border, she waits and whispers,
"Libertad."

No food or water
she's spent four days;
hitching rides, hiding underneath back seats,
stuffed in suffocating trunks,
hiked, ran, crawled, swam,
and had fevers of a 100, vomiting the little food she had in
chunks

A thousand yards from the US border, she waits and whispers,
"Libertad."

Surrounded by used syringes, coke bottles, torn clothes, and mis-
matching sneakers
the desert floor she sits on has become familiar with dream seek-
ers
Migrants call it a thousand yards of death, dream snatcher,
sun baker, soul taker.
She takes

the leftover torn clothes and wraps her bleeding pus foot

She inches forward and whispers, "Libertad."

Forward to country so backward.
A country birthed by immigrant Pilgrims whose children's children's children
will call her illegal, wetback, whore, slave, terrorist, beaner, job stealer
But she does not look back
for that is at least better than where she was at
poor, hungry, sick, uneducated
She inches forward towards the same country that has poisoned her oceans
where scriptures are being rewritten because God can't even teach a man to fish on that land
where factories are being built with no labor laws and 10 cents a day gets you five tuna cans
where her children pick days out of the week not to eat so their siblings can eat out that tuna
can
where farmers inject steroids in their livestock to compete in international markets to feed us
Americans
No! She won't turn back. She inches forward and whispers, "Libertad."
She inched forward, knowing one day
her future grandson would write a poem about a Dreamer
a dreamer who decades later fades at Bellevue Hospital.
Retired. Eyes lost coloration turned
grayish-blue. Lungs filled with fluids and a heart barely
beating. Foot swollen. She stares at me and mumbles, don't forget

44

me
A dreamer
who sacrificed everything
so that I
can have
"Libertad"

Uptown & The Bronx 1 2 3
UP·TOWN·TRAINS
Next stop
Uptown's Boogie Down
feast hometown buffet to
break beat that clog your
heart drums skip scratch
poetry over mics
powered by street lights
b-boys flip like
chicken wings on
cardboard boxes
graffiti paint bomb
sssssshhhhhhhhhh

BABY BIRDS

song bird

strapped words

to tungue

soul sung

from the

bottom lung

Towards the North

My ketchup on warm bread
Sweet sour salt sugar
Most men live dead
I'm not most men

I live to love you

Crunchy curvy edges
I place my pledges
at the center of your crust
trust

I won't fall apart like wheat crumb
and I would remain whole
in your warm hands
keep coming back
like bands rubberbands

I will not subtract your value
I will be the sum
and hum
like a bullet
towards the north

People of Color

Church Sunday

40 minutes before the rising sun
can peek its head down 149th street,
Sunday's waking up.
Few remained   un-tucked
through the Bronx
like empty plastic coke bottles
pushed towards the sea.

Baby powder showers his feet.
A gold jacket
dresses his lower teeth.
Freshly picked cotton   T-shirt
covers an unbeaten dark skin.

Eye's peer through St. Mary's project's
metaled   barred   windows
from the fourteenth floor.

The 2 Train injects the sound of
third rail and iron wheels
Clanking- Clanking- Clanking
off red brick buildings.

Chavo
wipes the babas from his son's lips
and kisses his eyebrows.
Eight months ago, his routine was easier.
Now
tucking Ruger into his True Religion jeans -
he grabs stacks of powder bundles,
tightly wrapped in aluminum foil,

and rubber bands.
Hundreds of dead presidents shepherd
into his back pockets.

A Jesus piece
hangs around his neck,
Chavo religiously kisses the diamond-encrusted crown
before he heads out towards the sanctuary.

Fiends await his presence
in front of Kennedy's Crown Chicken spot
the corner pulpit.

Smitty Smacks
arms with dried out tracks
will be the first in line   as usual
to receive his daily communion.
In the name of our four fathers
and for his son
Amen.

BURNING EYES

Don't cry
let

tonight go by
like fireflies

soon

stomach will cocoon

to free imprisoned butterflies

Over my Bowl of Cereal

Pour me
some milk
and honey

over my   cereooo
yo'
preacher man
gunner man
running out my window

plastic spoons
cover
silver moons
witness
roaches fight
over
rice crispy crumbs
in my bedroom
metal windows
guard visions
lockdown dreams
trap race relations
in prisms
light pop locks
to escape
empty fridges
minimum wage wars
poor me
St. Mary's
could you

Pour me

some milk
and honey

over my   cereooo
yo
preacher man
gunner man
running out my window

Bronx borough borrow bowls
to cut around afros
like the sun
after Jesus held up a church
on Sunday
at gunpoint
pastors replace bibles
with guns

In the name of capital
The Holy Dollar
Starved daughters and sons
A   man
broke bread dipped it in milk

Tish hides razor blades
in her box braids
to cut strangers
trying to climb on her mattress
like bed bugs who raid
intimate sheets
and leave un-washable print

crawling feet tickle hair
Tish's Meth Momma   don't care
if Simon says
if Simon says
if Simon says
touch here
touch there
who protects
St. Mary's children
under gun fire
burning bibles
Who protects the children of St. Mary's
too hot   to blow
over   my cereoo

Welcome

Welcome to Jackson Ave
home to greasy pigeons
who pocket crumbs
between their gums
stick up kids pop steel like bubble gum
bodega spots sell lemon heads
 and soda sperm killers at a discount

Brick rust buildings trump tower over horizon
Sun peek-o-boo morning
and the children of St. Mary's
get another day to rise

Cold Summer

Cold John
argued with No-Nonsense Benny
who was five years older

You think I'mah suckah?
Pero Johnny calma te

I watched through our
caged windows
Apt 13c

Where's the money, Benny?

I remembered
lightning bugs
not showing up that June.
This was the first time fireflies stood up St. Mary's.
They represented hope
and provided a little light to our darkness.

Sunday twelve am

Pero mira Johnny, I could fix this papi, lo tengo broderrr

Cold John and I were both
fourteen   muscular
dark-skinned trilingual mixed mutts
he was lighter
I was two inches taller

You can fix what? So the rest of these bum-asses could play me
out here… nah Sun!

I   a boxer undefeated in the olympics.
He   an up and coming crack cocaine dealer

Every summer
we were able to see hundreds of thousands of lightning bugs
light up our projects
Christmas in June

Dame otro chance Johnny, yo lo puedo 'reglar. For real papi, jus'
calm' down

Both   middle of the street
surrounded by a line of cars
Typically there's 100's of people
walking up and down Caudwell Avenue
playing Hector Lavoe Fat Joe
or Miles Davis
but tonight was light

Cold John swung one hand towards the back of his pants.

Kitchen and bedroom lights go black from Cold John's building
like an eclipse

Plackaaah

The first shot spits out a muzzled orange flash.
I ducked my head low
and turned off my bedroom lights

58

My brothers and mother ran into my room.

Plackaaah Plackaaaah

Papi please, please man, please

No Nonsense Benny's legs dragged towards Westchester Avenue

Plackaaah Plackaaaah Plackaaaah

Benny stopped moving.

Cold John patiently   lowered his gun.
He stared at the body.

New York street chatter ceased

only trains
buses   planes
cabs echoed
through the borough.

He slowly walked away
in his distinct Bx bop
A walk that distinguished he was calling the shots.

After that night
the lightning bugs never returned to St. Mary's.

RUN IT

at four
he draws
out from his torn coat pocket
wrinkled paper   oiled
by sleeping on concrete
in these St. Mary's street
a picture
stick figure
of his father
in a scribbled green house
with blue grass
under a purple bright sun
He kissed his forehead
told him   keep warm   I'll be
back Lil'Man
tucked his gun
and went on another run
eyo chill   chill   stand still

media paints
him a
moon-ster
block booster
night   star shooter
Saw Venus cry
from the reflection
of his blue steel
yo   yo   YO CHILL
CHILL sun   STAND STILL

He stole
Jesus from the cross
in exchange for his daily bread
of eighty-six dollars
deep fried chicken greased eggroll
a cup of sprite
and told
his son
take and drink
this is my sweat and blood
given on to you

I'M FROM

Rananchqua
Bronck's Place
Broncks
The Broncks
The Bronx
The BX
The Boogie Down
Uptown

That's how I Got It

When my father migrated to the Bronx
his favorite shopping center was
Alexanders.

Before:
>	the internet
>	Computers
>	Cell phones
>	Walmarts
>	Targets
there was

Alexanders.
He vowed to name his first born after . . .

My name is Alex

Abuelito throws on his blue baseball cap
Eyeballing an off white hallway
that splits between my mother's bedroom
and the door to freedom
which he called "La puerta de libertad"
I approached my grandfather puzzled like
          "Abuelito where you think you going?"
"Mira Carlo'"
"It's Alex Abuelito"
" Pero mira that's what I said,
mira look look look look look
vamos a escapar oye
today we escape Carlo'
"it's Alex Abuelito"
"I know Carlo, I know...
Tenemos que escapar from that crazy lady
oooh my Gawd
she just keeps feeding me
          and feeding me
          and feeding me
we gotta get outta here Carlo
"it's Alex Abuelito"
I know Carlo, I know
You're my only friend in the world

First People Too

Lenape villagers
bloody palms beaten backs
burried like plant seeds

If I could pull out some kicks
grey orange blue
I can slam dunk down the avenue
like Anthony Mason's Knicks
keep my soles tight
right
                    cuz
you don't want your feet
sticking out like tongues
flip flopping smacking
through the block
like chancla – chancla – chancla – chancla
Naaaah Sun!

        Dudes on the block
be calling your foot gear
Chatty Patty
Bum feet
Foots Of Horror
Walkie Talkies
Naah B'

        Keep your soles shut
listening to the crowded subways
during rush hour
clack – clack – doop – doop – slack – pat – pat
catching yellow cabs
Yo- Papi Papi how much for the Bronx Jackson Avenue
Busy bus stops
Cushioned toes
walking pass bodegas – liquor stores – and chicken spots
Chino, dame un wing large thigh con arroz y shrimp.. pero fo' real yo,
don't forget my duck sauce you tried to
        play me last week
Footwear should listen
 not speak
and keep the
dairies of our streets
stitched into
their soles

Just For Kicks

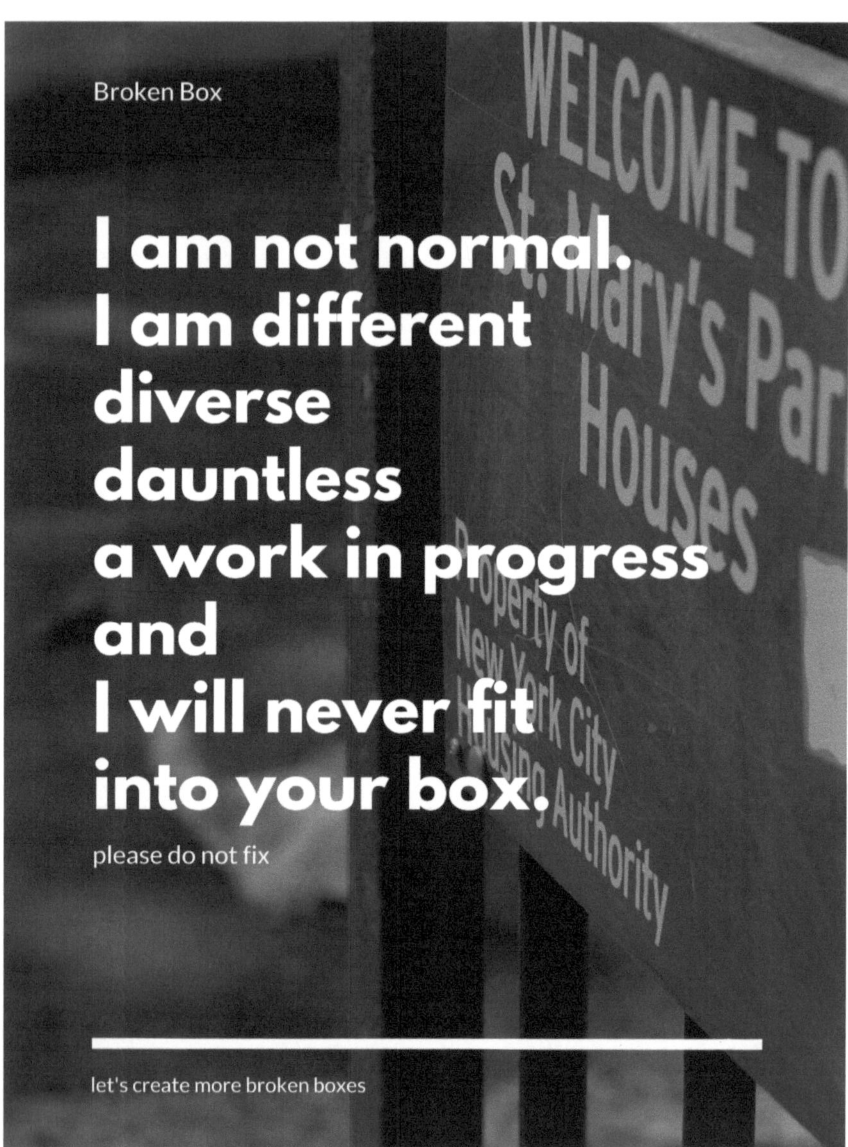

Broken Box

I am not normal.
I am different
diverse
dauntless
a work in progress
and
I will never fit
into your box.

please do not fix

let's create more broken boxes

Danny died when we were young

we were just kids   I did not attend his funeral

he was one of my best friends and my mother treated him like a son

now I walk pass his mural

8·20·78 / 1·28·95
Rest In Peace
Danny

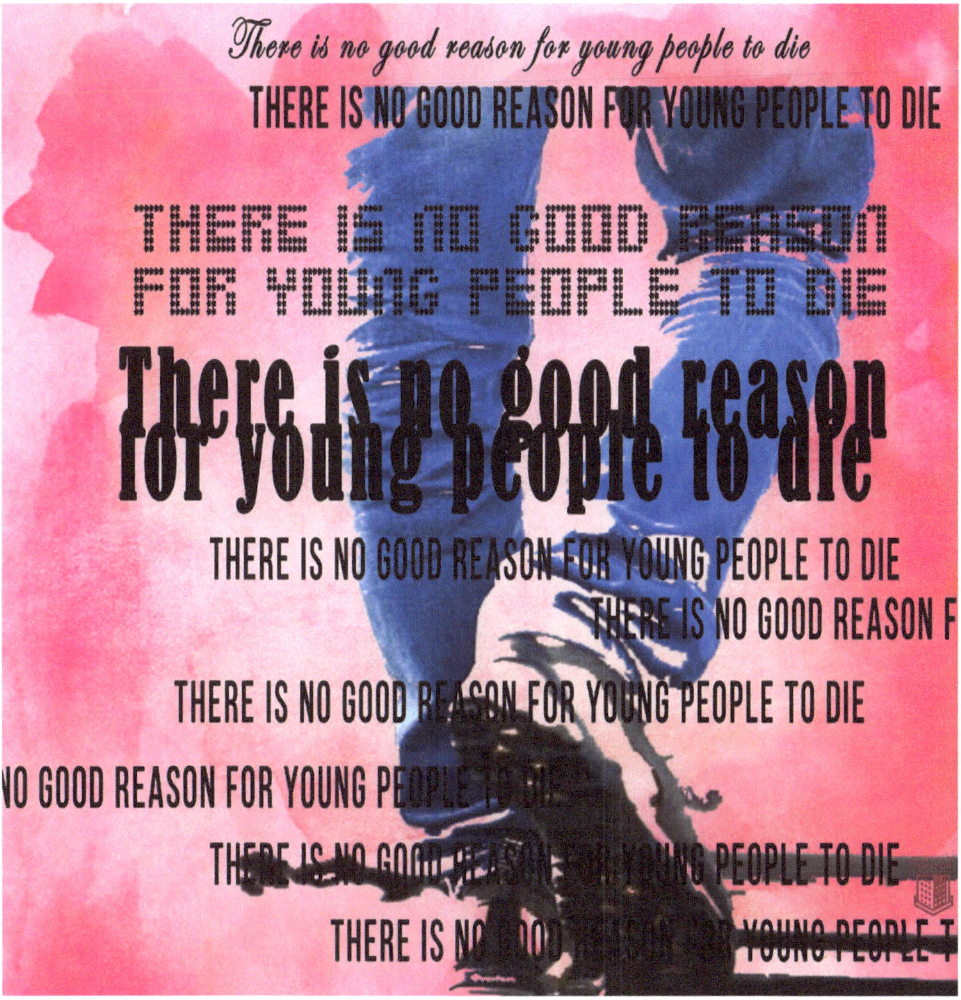

There is no good reason for young people to die
THERE IS NO GOOD REASON FOR YOUNG PEOPLE TO DIE
THERE IS NO GOOD REASON FOR YOUNG PEOPLE TO DIE
There is no good reason for young people to die
THERE IS NO GOOD REASON FOR YOUNG PEOPLE TO DIE
THERE IS NO GOOD REASON F
THERE IS NO GOOD REASON FOR YOUNG PEOPLE TO DIE
NO GOOD REASON FOR YOUNG PEOPLE TO DIE
THERE IS NO GOOD REASON FOR YOUNG PEOPLE TO DIE
THERE IS NO GOOD REASON FOR YOUNG PEOPLE T

Best Grade

Ms. Madera
1st grade teacher
laughed
when I told the class
I want to be a writer.

A Puerto Rican brunet
who lost her accent
in the Atlantic.

You need to work
on your English.
Almost every homework
assignment you bring in
is incorrect. She scolded.

I never told her
my father sat with me
every night to help me
with my homework.
Those were the best F's
I've ever gotten.
My writing wasn't
any good anyway.

A Day At A Time

6 days
21 hours
Smitty Smacks
hasn't touch
a bottle   pipe or needle
since his sister's funeral

Levy attended
all her brother's races
at South Bronx High

Two years younger
confined to a wheel chair   at birth
She wore her brother's legs in her mind

Levy was the first one to notice
how her brother   padded his own back
when he lapped   his opponents

I counted eight Smitty
You slapped your back eight times
and came in first place
Tell'em Smitty, Tell'em that you really did pat your back

Sam Smith blushed   put his sister on his back
ran a victory lap   with Levy yelling
Go Smitty Smacks – Go Smitty Smacks – Gooo

A decade later
he stares at a watch
he brought from Freddy Flip Time
sweating shaking in an abandon shack

rocking to the sound of his sister's chant
trying to beat his addiction
tracing the tracks on his arms
waiting for the seventh day to come
so that he could pat his back
6 days   23 hours
Go Smitty Smacks – Go Smitty Smacks – Gooo

Site Splash

Out my window
St. Mary's playground
huddled by green trees

where laughter echoed
cement rainbow barrels

shells fell empting barrels

B-boys spun heads
on cardboard spreads
front back flip suicides

Smitty Smacks lit pipe
flew like purple kite
colors swurl skin like tie - dyed

Sassy Sandy double dutched
smacked gum like
feet to concrete
with the lightest touch

Tevin practiced his crossover
/ 3 point clutch

Ceelo dice tossed over
dead presidents
second quarter
passed to Coquito-Lady

Pigeons ate left over
pizza dough

same place
Chavo use to
count his dough

Concrete
Jungle
Gym

no speak ingle

Le dehe que no speak ingle
Le dehe que no speak ingle
Yo solo speak
En la lengua de la trumpeta
Para ta ta para ta ta

That's not how you say that
It's not Catchu
it's Ketchup
Ketchup man ketchup
Catch up

El trompetista seem'd unfazed
He laughed at the English speaker
and said, "Mira tu tiene que catchup, me entiéndes."

Pan tan tan pan tan

La trumpeta split syllables
like Peas in a pot
Salsa hot
Spicy paprika

Pan tan tan pan tan

Yo no espeak ingle
Yo espeak
Tah tan tan tan tah

The trumpet spoke jazz funk
Mambo
It was

It is   multi-lingo

Pan tan tan pan tan

The English speaker shook his head
disappointed   he really wanted to help
the Trumpet player learn to speak proper
in this America
El trompetista   30 years older than the teenager
A young man with his digital music
First generation born on US soil

Elevator Chatter

They found his body
behind the red metal door
      with white letters that read
      EXIT.
Bullet lodged in his afro.
His afro pick's fist emblem broken pieces
scattered across the cement stairs
of the second floor.

They said he was trying to run
the way they found his face
faced down.

His front teeth missing,
covered in urine and blood.

His eyes were still open.
His shinny brown skin pale
dry.

His blood ran down towards the lobby.
St. Mary's held on to him 'til ambulance
cops came stepping over clues.

I was nine in the elevator headed
towards the 20th floor,
afraid to cry among the crowded metal box.

He was a Junkie someone bragged.
A damn bum another exclaimed.
Never did anything with his life.

I said nothing.
I was the last to get off the elevator,
pulled out my keys.

Walked down the yellow tiled hallway.
I stared at the green metal door that read
apartment #20G.	He was my neighbor.
He was my best friend.

Day Two
p2

Smitty Smacks
stares across tracks
peeling pus back
watching blood
drip iron
his sister's laughter
flat ironed
starched
stitched into
stomach
steam
leaves cotton tongue
thirsting for another hit

Frontin' On The 4 Line

Iron Horse   crowded
4pm rush hour
The Four Line

Tish African Plum
TAP TAP
On my chest like native drums

149st
train tilts sharp turns
We smile
like lemon heads on a third grader's tongue
starburst melts in hand
The galaxy between our teeth.

A freshmen in high school
making his first move

Yo Shortie, ain't you fr'm Mr. Seeger's math class - I ask.

Her friend who could smell the Bronx off of my jeans says,

Oooh, I know you ain't trynna holla at my friend.
Tish don't talk to him   he wanna' them Bronx Boys

mo' like Bronx Bums
You know that Harlem Brooklyn and Queens girls don't talk to them
Rowdy wild crazy dirty no-class-having no-home-training boys.

Dreams   crushed like ice in a cup
Piragua coconut special.
Tish African Plum was special.
Bodies crammed like sardines.
We smiled as people piled into the iron horse.

Her box braids went passed her gold chain initialed TH.
Her deep red lips matched the blood that ran through my neck.
Her faint Jamaican British accent mixed with a Harlem swang
pounded through my chest like a fist of an orangutan.
The damage was done. Tish and I never spoke again.
with quiet stares on a 4 train.

Permanent strangers
Next stop 149 street Yankee Stadium, stand clear for closing doors.

Preacher Man's Daughter

Preacher Man's daughter
opens door
to pitch blue night.
St. Mary's sirens howl
towards the softball yellow moon.
Walking to the ledge
of a 21st story building.
Summer breeze crawls up
a stained purple short skirt.

She yells off
        the ledge of a 21st story building
I'm not your daughter?
What do I have to do for you to love me.

She screams at St. Mary's

We fell in love with her
the moment she appeared
She was loud, bright-eyed
and had no fear
Many said she would die
Before her fifth birthday
She celebrates her 40th
Hip Hop all night and day.

NY
THE
COOL
KIDS
CLUB

The
Know

I don't hate, nor do I resent my past. I appreciate the good and bad, for they shape the principals I stand on today. The future only makes sense if I bring all these experiences on the journey.

Alex Avila
Professor, Poet,
Author, Advocate

BRICK CITY
BLOCK
BY
BLOCK

WE ALL WENT TO SHOP   TO CHOP CHOP   SOME OFF THE SIDE   AND OFF THE TOP   IT WAS ONE OF THOSE SACRED   PLACES ON THE BLOCK

African drums penetrated her walls shook her bones
She wanted to marry the music
and never   be alone

BARBER TALK
BEST MCEES
KRS-ONE
FAT JOE
REMY MA
COREY GUNZ
THE LOX
FRED THE GODSON
GRANDMASTER CAZ
MYSONNE
CARDI B
MELLE MEL
DMX
SLICK RICK
BIG PUN
FRENCH MONTANA

She Keeps Passing Me, Bye

The only time I catch the wind
is within the pocket's of my skin

Stalked like the sun
chest drum
heard her breathe

Talked to trees
they say
she can come and go as she pleases.

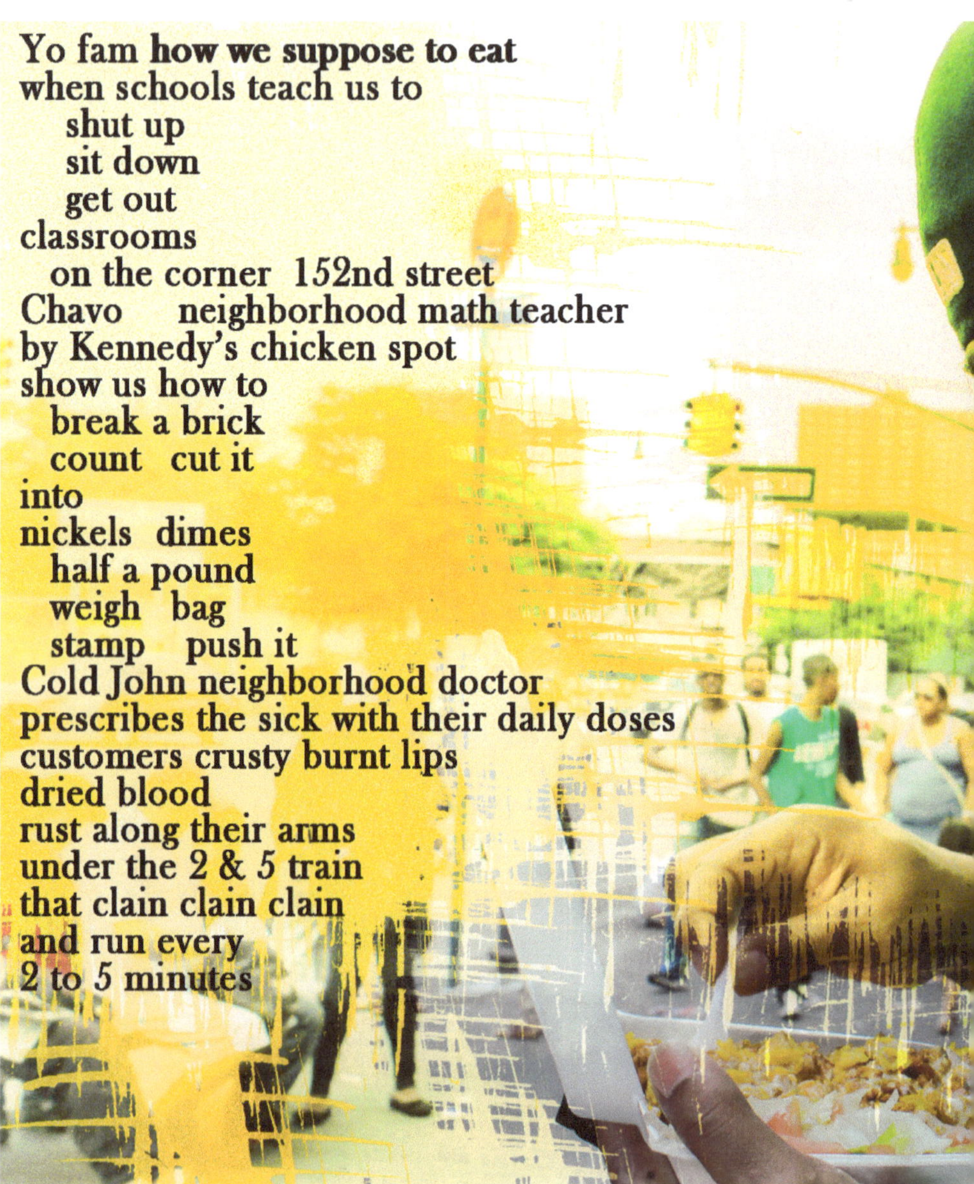

Yo fam **how we suppose to eat**
when schools teach us to
   shut up
   sit down
   get out
classrooms
  on the corner 152nd street
Chavo   neighborhood math teacher
by Kennedy's chicken spot
show us how to
   break a brick
   count   cut it
into
nickels dimes
   half a pound
   weigh   bag
   stamp   push it
Cold John neighborhood doctor
prescribes the sick with their daily doses
customers crusty burnt lips
dried blood
rust along their arms
under the 2 & 5 train
that clain clain clain
and run every
2 to 5 minutes

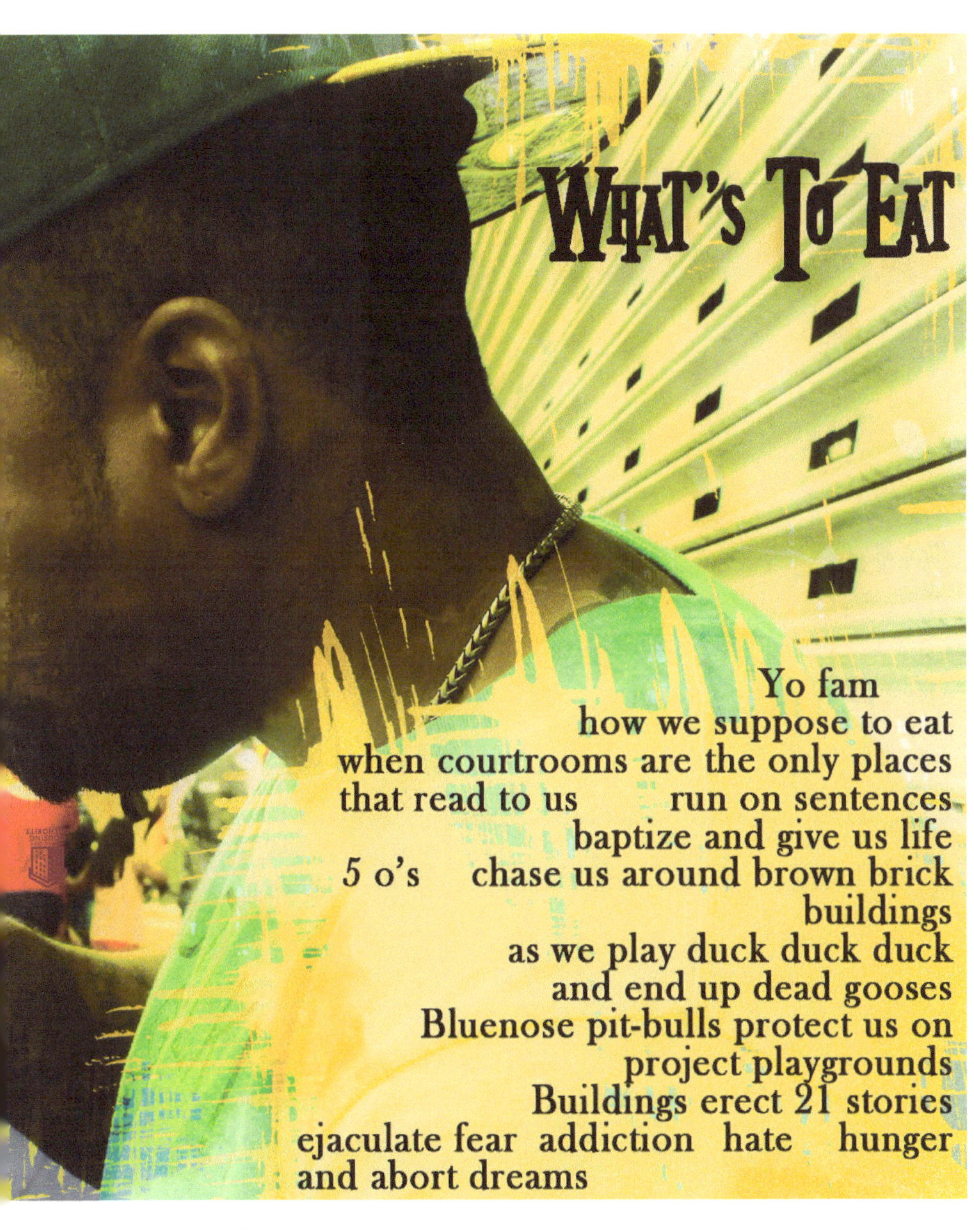
WHAT'S TO EAT

Yo fam
how we suppose to eat
when courtrooms are the only places
that read to us   run on sentences
baptize and give us life
5 o's   chase us around brown brick
buildings
as we play duck duck duck
and end up dead gooses
Bluenose pit-bulls protect us on
project playgrounds
Buildings erect 21 stories
ejaculate fear addiction hate   hunger
and abort dreams

Making Moves

HOLEY SOCKS BIG TOE OF DREAMS HELP ME STEP IN THE RIGHT DIRECTION

Don't just stand there, make a move!

Gata Lady p2

Si mi amor, ya voy.. ya voy
She says as Fila purrs

She gets up
Coughing lightly
into balled fist

massages scar
 across chest

Drags each foot
scratches right missing ear
out of habit
just pieces of meat
leftover
from when
a football-sized rat
bit it off
she was 11 then

Sixty years later

Opens black metaled   barred
window
to breathe in St. Mary's
pigeon pooped
burned menthol
cab   bus fumes
cool water perfume
Olay hair spray
From her second-story
Apartment

A gush of brisk wind
lets itself in
an apartment stack
with books
newspapers
followed by lobby chatter
Yo kid
The Knicks did their thing b'
Cabs honking at children
Blocking lanes
Freddy Fox yells from a long brown bench,
"Ey – yo Gata Lady
come feed your children
they are meowing me to death
for Chrissake"
She hisses back
walks into the second bedroom screaming
          Sandy levantate, you're gonna be late mija
Gata Lady heads into the kitchen to fill a bag with burnt rice
for the pigeon
and old milk for the kitties
Sandy levantate, no necesito tu escuela que me llamen
let's go, mija let's go
four cats circle Gata lady's feet
waiting for yesterday's leftovers

Tracking

Rowdy Rod   use to
slap my back
with a yellow aluminum bat
under these iron tracks
cracked
my Black skin open
bled on   nice whites
ran up
fourteen flights
soaked my face in the mirror
eyelids swelled with terror
Mind swam with vengeance
    One day I'mah kick your a$$

Decades later
on the 2train
Rowdy Rod didn't even remember
my name
his name
head slowly swung front to back
30 mph on the tracks
He drooled on his lap
guilt entrapped in my synapse
old thoughts collapse
inside coco-buttered palms
to see Rowdy Rod
strung out
on crack

Don't
Die

Tevin's Bedroom Plastered

Officer Oreb aims his gun
at a 90° angle
from shoulder to elbow
blue uniform
wrinkles in position
Tevin stares in aaaw
processed curly black hair 'laxed
almond skin
wrapped in teenage musk
Oreo scented fingers
grips denim tight
Officer Oreb's pale left hand
turns off his walkie
gun rises at 120°
       Tevin's forearm muscle
       tense
       cotton shirt
       collects sweat
Officer Oreb puts gun closer to face
closes right blue eye
index massages trigger
       Tevin's pimpled face glistened
       a virgin
       obsess with basketball
       and video games
Officer Oreb pulls the trigger
they both scream
laugh
at zombies heads bursting
like watermelons
falling from the fifth floor
Tevin grabs the orange gun

From Officer's Oreb
Oreb pats Tevin's head and says
I'll buy you more video games
if you keep up the good grades in school.
Oreb
an Irishmen
who has adopted all of St. Mary's children.

Street Hunger
Sneakers
chew gums
with no
sole

Despasito

Despasito mi negra va bilando
Va bilando.   Por la noche

Sea salt seasons her skin
the color of   x3

Despasito mi negra va bilando
Va bilando.   Por la noche

Cocoa and coffee bean
hips shake
Shake. Shake.   Shake
like powdered nutmeg
Everyday's a holiday

Despasito mi negra va bilando
Va bilando.   Por la noche

My grandmother
dancing by the ocean
caressing a full moon   with her fingers
Her fingers   her fingers
smell like coconut water
This is before my father
would marry her daughter
when she danced by the ocean water
Dreaming
Dreaming of America
A dreamer dreaming if America
when America
how America

Despasito mi negra va bilando
Va bilando.   Por la noche

Starfishes
glitter her reflection
She's a traffic jam
in any direction

This is before the detention centers
Before deportation
Before the water turned ice
Before working 16 hours days. Taking care of the rich
Before the nightmares

There was a dream
A Dreamer
dancing by the pacific
Smile as white as sea shells

Despasito mi negra va bilando
Va bilando.   Por la noche

Today

No dead bodies
No fights

Laughter carousel's
Prism lights

Evening dreaming
of St. Mary's

In prison
she stays up
all night
wondering   if her
four year old
still calls her name

The Boots That Never Came Off

When shots shouted
     against his brown brick building
       Willie flung his two hundred and 30   pound
Black body
Black body
   in a military crawl
underneath a frameless mattress

Grey tiled floor
crouched miles away from his window
unable to hear the city's yellow cabs
trains   planes
Black body Black body Black bodies
Pee pa peee pah Pee pa peee pah
      Pee pa peee pah
         Papapapapapapapapapaaaaah

He hummed
whispered sung
a trait picked up in Kuwait
Afghanistan Iraq

after his friend Murder Mack
shot in the back
fell right into Willie's arm
Murder Mack laughing singing crying

You gotta turn it into music
It's the only way to survive
And if you're gonna die
go out signing Damn It!
Imagine all the people living in this world he he ...

His eyes mouth wide open staring right at Willie
Still still still Black body   underneath frameless mattress
                  Now   Willie
grips
     a Smith & Wesson SIG P229 semi –auto
      from the fifth floor of St. Mary's projects

Pee pa peee pah Pee pa peee pah

Rocking back and forth
peeking through burlap curtains
and is unaware he's in the Bronx

Papapapapapapapapapaaaaah

Echo Knocking on my Window

I lived on the 20th floor
of St. Mary's project.
       Don't remember
when we moved there
from Harlem.
I recall
gunshots
echoed pass my bedroom
window.
I was five
trying to squeeze
my head through
black metal bars.
I pressed my ear
towards the Bronx warm air.
No screams.
Couldn't find
a sound to follow
or that belong to the
bullets.
Mañana I'll hunt
para los shells.

Next Stop

St. Mary's Ride

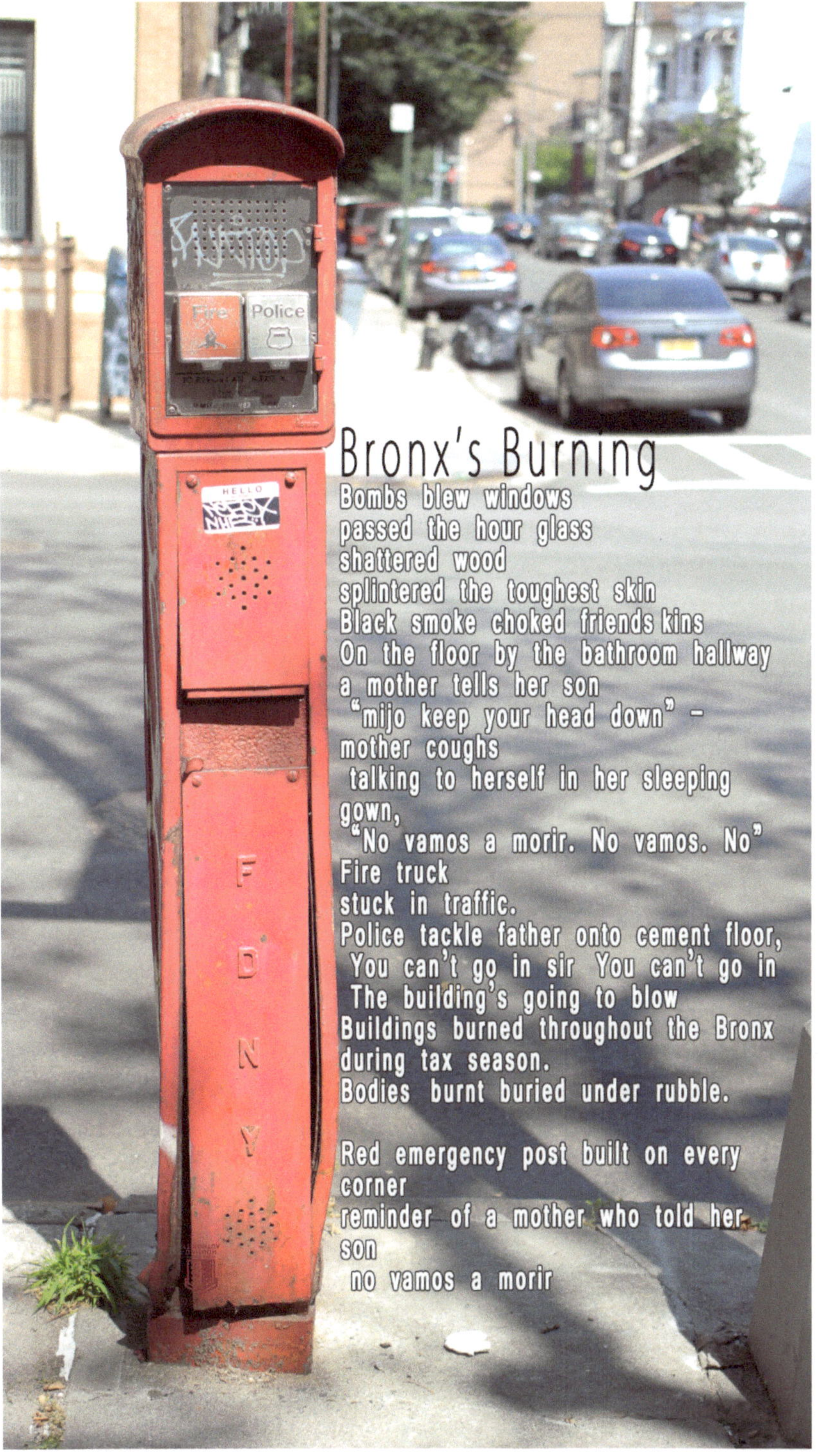
Bronx's Burning
Bombs blew windows
passed the hour glass
shattered wood
splintered the toughest skin
Black smoke choked friends kins
On the floor by the bathroom hallway
a mother tells her son
"mijo keep your head down" –
mother coughs
 talking to herself in her sleeping
gown,
"No vamos a morir. No vamos. No"
Fire truck
stuck in traffic.
Police tackle father onto cement floor,
 You can't go in sir You can't go in
 The building's going to blow
Buildings burned throughout the Bronx
during tax season.
Bodies burnt buried under rubble.

Red emergency post built on every
corner
reminder of a mother who told her
son
 no vamos a morir

2

Tracking
Time
Iron horses
gallop through
St. Mary's
whirligig the Bronx

The days
their bodies sprayed
with aerosol
skin bombed
with murals
tattooed in street ads

those were the days
Stallion
those were the days

An Angel is Coming

Tienes que comer
Mami begged

Abuelo forgets everything
He calls Mami   la mala bruja
                       ella siempre veine
                       con su escoba en una mano
                       y sopa en la otra
                       y le dece
que coma, que coma, que coma
Abuelito remembers grandma though.
He called her   the most beautiful specimen in the world.
They fought like cats and birds.
Abuelo was more like a penguin trying to swim away
from granny's swinging broom and an occasional butcher's knife.
He loves granny.   He forgets to eat,
put on his pants,
my mother's name
But not what he used to sing to granny.

Coro:
Que bien te ves... que chevere
Que bien te ves.

Abuelo got up and two step in front of the kitchen window
singing   swinging his fragile hips
his knees wobbled
He stayed on beat.
Tap tap tap   tap tap
Tap tap tap   tap tap   on his chest stomach
                       He tapped his body

114

with his wrinkled hands
Tap tap tap   tap tap

Abuelo forgets everything but not the beautiful lady.
Granny passed decades ago.
I remember when she was sick
Abuelo would be by her side crying   singing.
Que bien te ves... que chevere
Que bien te ves.

Granny's body swollen   skin tight with water
Eyes buzzed with heavy drugs.
The diabetes was eating her toes.
Wheezing for air
Abuelo sat next to her in his wooden chair
Que bien te ves... que chevere
Que bien te ves

Whipping tears from her eyes.
He talked about the blue dress she wore by the beach in Bahamar.
How the starfish envied her glow.
How Honduras would never forgive the man who took their one
true angel.
Que bien te ves... que chevere
Que bien te ves

He forgot my name and called me Carlo
Carlo was his best friend he grew up with in Honduras.

Carlo apurate mis pantalones   I am going to see my angel.

Tap tap tap   tap tap

Tap tap tap   tap tap   on his chest   stomach
                              He tapped his body
with his wrinkled hands
Tap tap tap   tap tap

Carlo, my Angel is coming for me. So no se que te decer catracho
Pero brother me tengo que ir. Catrocho me tengo que ir de aqui.

This was my grandfather saying goodbye to all of us,
whoever we were.

I got him his fancy blue pants that match my granny's dress
when they met by the ocean.

We will be okay Abuela, we'll be okay. I said.

We sang together in the kitchen of St. Mary's project.
I was the one singing to him now.
I was singing for all of us.
Que bien te ves... que chevere
Que bien te ves

Eh... que bien, que bien,
que bien, que bien tu te ves.

116

Mami says

I stood
on the kitchen table
next to a wide open
window.
I was three
with a blanket
tied around my neck.
Warm afternoon
deep blue sky.
From the 20th floor
I screamed, "Yo soy superrrman."
        "Si mijo." She says nervously.
There were no bars on the windows.
        Yo soy superrrman. I screamed
jumping on the table.
        Si mijo, eres Superman. She says
walking slowly towards me.

Years later
she stressed over the phone
how dozens of children died
every year. Housing felt it was an
unnecessary expense
to place metal bars along
the windows. She laughs
recalling my chant . . .
        Yo soy superrrman, Mami. I sat on
the rocky table with foldable metal legs.
My legs were moving towards the window.
Arms were stretched towards the deep blue . . .
        Yo brinque, y te agarré del estómago. Pero que me dio un
susto

Laughter bursts out the other end of the phone.
Mami was the true hero
my mother was the real Superman.

mothers Broom
children's crayon

Building vision
gusty winds
Plaster Dandelions
upon Brown Bricks
children graffiti
cement building
with green red blue
crayola wax
while mothers sweep
dope needles
Broken Beer Bottles
aside
so little junior
could finish writing
I love you
St. Mary's Project

A Is For Alien

Robert leans over.
Ms. Johnson writes alphabets
on a green chalkboard.
Pssst, pssst, pssst. Hey.
I turn in a wooden chair
with a curious stare.
Robert's finger-pointing at me
and says,
Your daddy's   an alien.
I was six
when I found out my daddy was an alien.
I would get up
watch my daddy brush his teeth,
waiting for his skin to turn green,
hair to fall out.
See aliens sail in ships
    aliens sail in ships
land in the U   S   A
and kidnap children.
It's true,
I saw it in a movie.
Papele Papele Papele
Pa pa pa papales.
I sneak behind him in the kitchen
pretend to play with my red Hot Wheels racer
waiting for his eyes
to turn completely black
like a Bronx tunnel tucking trains and rats.
He was a good actor,
flipping cinnamon pancakes
like a normal person.
I was six when I found out.

My daddy's an alien.
Papele Papele Papele
Pa pa pa papales.
Aliens are illegal.
Aliens are illegal.
They kidnap children
steal their eyes
and swallow their skins.
Whenever he came to hug me
I flinched.
The hairs on my almond skin stood up.
When he patted my head
I jumped.
Is he gonna snatch my skin off my bones,
RIP MY EYEs OFF MY SOCKET?
We don't need walls.
We need Superdome
to keep the aliens out
and the only way to get in
is with special IDs and papers.
Does mami know?
Is she an alien too?
Papele Papele Papele
Pa pa pa papales.
I was six
scared of werewolves, vampires
and aliens.
I was six
waking up at 3   4   5
in the morning
checking eyes and skin.
Papele Papele Papele
Pa pa pa papales.

Hombre y Paloma

Night lights glimmer jealously
blackout stars.
Moon tucked in clouds.
An Immigrant Bird
crashes into a Macy's building
        off 52nd street,
lands a couple of yards from Babbito's bottle
Spat   bap bop throp
tries to hop   back in flight.

Yellow cars   roooooar
        down grey roads
with white tattoos,
lines that end at the Atlantic.
Frantic
shoes clack clack clacking off walls,
boots clunker.
Chatter moves nowhere and everywhere
there's glowing pocket machines.

Bobbito removes several blankets off
of him.
Leans over   to watch
an Immigrant Bird
bap bop throp
trying to hop back in flight
its beak rest
tired   against concrete.

Bobbito blows warm air
into gloves with cutout fingertips.
He puts his bottle on a step   five feet deep
by a door filled with
122

shadows   that haven't open in decades,
piled with black plastic bags.
He gets up   drags
his right foot
towards the Immigrant Bird trying to . . .

        Bobbito takes off one of his gloves
and blankets the limping
bap bop throp
trying to hop back in flight.

Kneeling on his blankets
Bobbito wraps the immigrant
        in a Macy's scarf.
Cracks open a sunflower seed
smashes it to bits
and with its first feed
        Bobbito says
Welcome to my home

Solar

Before Seven   Tevin

Fire flicks
dance topless wicks
Wax licks
to glass bottle sticks
Tevin's pic
sits
among
flowers
candles lit
Carzzzz
Buzzzz
busy   strip

sixteen
be-   gun
popping zits
Pigeons blitz
fallen sun
bullet zipped
through afro pic
wolly hair part
like Moses's stick
skin
skull
split
like witnesses
who want
nothing
 to do
with it

Help me

Echoed
On building's
Burgundy bricks
21 stories
but this
kept
tight-lipped
fifteen pass six
Iron horse whipped
through Jackson Avenue
Turn twist
Corner
From St. Mary's projects
Blood
on Jordan kicks
leaked
from Tevin's lips

Please
help me

brown pupil
race
with wisdom
short snipped
     black fist
     loosened grip
     holding Nacho Cheese
Dorito chips
body laid
stretched

like Lady Liberty
floating
        the Atlantic

Mothers grab children
frantic
A homeless man
drops a cigarette
unlit
Cabs run red lights
Bus Driver
slams
shuts
door
Yells   HEADS DOWN PLEASE SIT
Shooter 22
        Bullet nest
        in cerebellum
        black hand
        blue fingertips

Tevin bathes in his own blood
        Reaching towards Jackson Ave to

        Please   help me

26 seconds
        Count   down
parents whose bloodline
stream the Montego Bay
let go
honor rolls

basketball trophies
point guard of the year
plaques
that stack
underneath Iverson's poster
planes that soar above giant buildings
Lisa's love poem wrinkled
    tucked
    in back of blue jean pocket
    Tevin bleeds out
    begging St. Mary's
    if he could have another
    shot

A TASTE OF LIBERTY
Freddy Flip Time

Hey lady
I'm selling liberty
2 for ten
Freedom in a bottle
This has the power to heal
Depression
Writers block
Dehydration
Bad breath

e-yo check this out
it's also
calorie and gluten free
guarantee or your money back
only for the last part though

But it looks like regular water

Don't get it confused
This is organic
from lady liberty herself.
Her aura has dissolved with the minerals
in this bottle
for the last 200 years   on my granny.
Freedom in a bottle is filled
with liberation content.
I should charge twenty a bottle
but you look like you need permission to be free
and I gotchu right here see
Fat free guarantee or your money back

Red Bottoms

He pushed her into the iron horse.
She fell forward.
Her head missing a metal pole
by a foot.

Stand clear for closing doors,
          announced an automated conductor.

She tried screaming.
He jumped on her back
wrapped a towel around her mouth.

4 am a quiet downtown Manhattan

She knew not to go to the back
and take the last train cart
especially after 2 am
on a slow Sunday morning
no one's ever there

Her   here
buried under a transit tunnel
made of steel cement iron . . .
She tried to scream again.
He threw a brunt blow
to her right ribcage.

It was late. She was visiting her cousin Chavo
whose son was in the hospital
with a fever of a 104.
Chavo hated Lincoln hospital in the Bronx.

130

Her   here   hear
He spun her around wildly to her stomach.
The iron horse sped up.
Her fingers dug deep into his cheekbone
        tore flesh   white meat exposed.
He screamed under his grey hood.
Yellow skinned middle-aged man
He weighed about a teenager and a half
on a varsity team.

Native's know   middle train carts are safer after hours.
They're closer to staircases
to cops.

They wrestled on dry dirt
greasy   pissy floor.
He backed hand her   while
she tried to snatch his eyes off his skull.

Chavo begged her to wait. He was going to
take her home back home to St. Mary's.
        I'mah big girl. I ain't worried about these losers
        Y tu no eres mi papa Chavo ya ta dehe, so calm down
        I gotta be at work at 8
        She said, eyes half-sleep.
Chavo thanked her for coming to the hospital.

Her   here   hear   how
he went to strike her again.
She kneed him in his groin.
His hands immediately consoled his penis, Shhhit.
She kneed him again.

The Iron Horse rocked their bodies back and forth.

He fell over, moaning in tears.
She rushed to her feet
kicking him in the face.
He screamed   No stop, stop, please.

        I'm from the Bronx Bitch
        and Sela Bela's my name motherfuc . . .
        she yelled, kicking him repeatedly.

Hear   her   here   now
her Timberland stiletto boots were bathed in blood.
She spat on his face.

Iron Horse stopped—doors open.
This is a Manhattan-bound Bronx express train
          announced the automated conductor.
She stumbled off the train cart holding her side.
Stand clear for closing doors.

Jackson AV
Westchester Avenue
as
Tevin's body posted
on this street corner
chalked by coroners
sneaker's soles
walk pass
old blood
screams still
sealed
in pavement
We Walk
Passed the Past

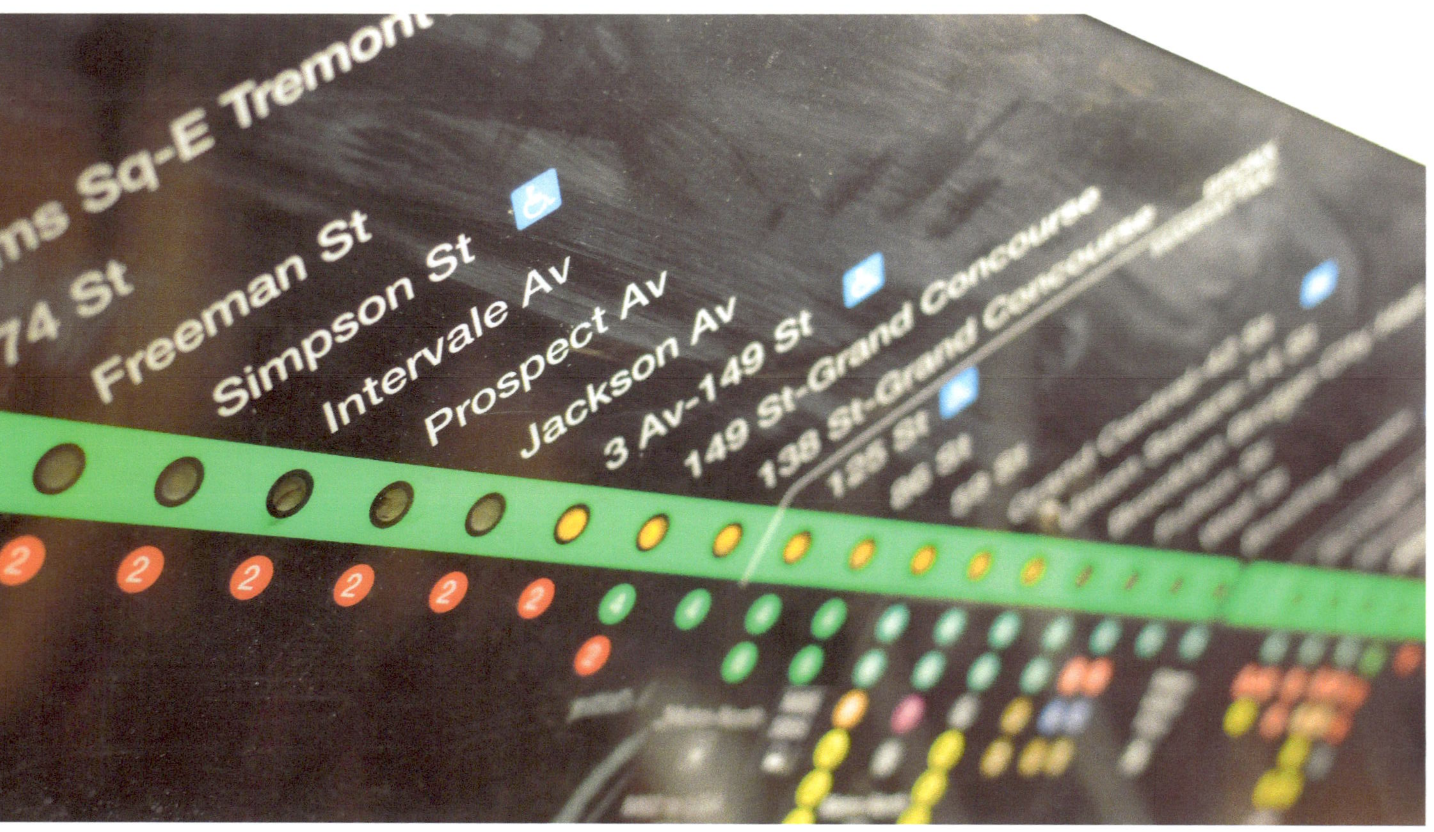
ms Sq-E Tremont
74 St
Freeman St
Simpson St
Intervale Av
Prospect Av
Jackson Av
3 Av-149 St
149 St-Grand Concourse
138 St-Grand Concourse
125 St

Dear St. Mary's Project.

Thank you for the knuckle balled fist fights in your graffiti'd cement stairwells. I was ten then with a nappy headed bowl cut. I was eighty pounds wet when Rowdy Rod knocked me down. Rowdy Rod two years older. spat on my food in your community center. Rowdy Rod took a plastic yellow bat after school smacking my neck - shoulders - back all the way to you. Yellow bucktooth. Wooly black hair. Acme caked face. Dusty brown skin and a foot taller than me . . . yeah that's him. Rowdy Rod. Chased me up your 21 flights 'til I pulled the ohkeedoke. I ran up and down your staircases. You watched as Rowdy Rod smack my strawberry Push-Pop from my hand and stomp on it. You watched but you knew.

You knew that Sunday afternoon. on the seventeenth floor. when Rowdy Rod pushed me down halfway towards the sixteenth floor that I would get back up. You were holding me as best as you could. Just us three. you. Rowdy Rod. and me. I stopped running. I dragged myself up swinging. biting. kneeing. and kicking. I stopped running. Rowdy Rod screamed Help Stop Jesus Please. and accidently tripped over my foot landing on his butt.   My knuckles balled fist tight. mouth drooling with anger Come On Parate. Because of you. I stopped running. I never stopped getting up after that.

I haven't seen Rowdy Rod since. Thank you so much St. Mary's. Sincerely.

Trinity Av

I read

between the lines, around the lines, master to cross the lines in order to get the baton to the finish line.

Alex Avila

SCHOOL BUS
10434
1-800-336-3886
ATLANTIC EXPRESS

Knock

Over 500 people live
in one buidling in St. Mary's.
There are four buildings on one block-
do the math.

St. Mary's Stepchild

keep cover
lay low
picaninni nap
sleep deep poppy root
shoot   weeds
grow   blow
like Dandelions
in a Jasmine spring breeze
invasive species
imported aliens
skin colored tone treated
like   feces
eye's caramel colored reese's

Choco   late
Baby boom bloom
Bees pollinate
Souls that hung rung
dripped under sun color rum
crawl like crab grass

stripped stripe flag
sewn with fresh cotton

Trust.

THE BEAUTY
AMONG US.

OWN YOUR PERCEPTION INVEST IN
YOURSELF-FAMILY-COMMUNITY.

Ghetto Antebellum
Screenplay

Alex Avila

EXT. ST. MARY'S PARK BENCH CINCO sneaks a stare at LA BRUJA from the bench. LA BRUJA on the other side of the bench talking to her friends. FRESCO sits next to CINCO.

                    FRESCO
          What's good-sucker for love?

                    CINCO
          Fall back sun. You buggin'.

                    FRESCO
          I see Bruja got another suspect
          under her spell. You staring so
          hard you probably got glaucoma.

                    CINCO
          (throwing a playful punch)
          It ain't even like that. I know
          shorty. We went to school together.
          You know.

                    FRESCO
          No, I don't, and if that's the truth
          why don't you just go over there and
          say what's up? (beat) Yeah, my point
          exactly. Anyway, she's off the books.
          Dating her would start another war.

                    CINCO
          You're buggin'. No I am not in love
           or trapped in some spell. For the
           record B',

144

it never crossed my mind to ask her
out. I was just . . .

                FRESCO
Damn shame, brother's always front
when it comes to love.

                CINCO
Who said I was . . .

                FRESCO
We're taught to hate like it's some
man thing but the manliest thing you
could do is fall in love. I fall in
love with every girl I meet. It's a
natural high; better than crack -
meth- cocaine . . .

                CINCO
Didn't you just say falling in love
is for suckers?

                FRESCO
No! The only suckers are the ones who
do not take advantage of love. You
just can't fall in love with La Bruja
because it will break the peace
between the projects. Her brother's
a psychopath and the only thing he
loves is his sister.

EXT.LA BRUJA'S FRIEND SOLA walks over to CINCO
and FRESCO.

                    SOLA
Bruja wants to ask you a question.

                  FRESCO
Sorry beautiful we were just
leaving. Tell shorty . . .

                  CINCO
Naw, I'm good. I'll go see what's
up.

                  FRESCO
                (Alarmed)
Yo fam what you . . .

                  CINCO
            (giving FRESCO a hard stare)
Ain't nobody shook over here,(beat)
I'll be over shortie. Let me chop it
up with man real quick. (SOLA nods
her head and walks back to LA BRUJA)

                  FRESCO
I was just playin' bro. You don't
need to take this any further. You
win.

                  CINCO
Sun, I already told you. It ain't
even like that. Relax bro. It's
just a question.

    EXT. As CINCO walks over to LA BRUJA her

brother walks over at the same time.

                    LA BRUJA
          So what, you just goin' to stare
          at me all day?

                     CINCO
          Woooow! You serious?

     EXT.LA BRUJA's brother RAYMOND runs behind
CINCO who is unaware.
                    RAYMOND
          Yooo what the . . .

To be continued . . .

MY ADDICTION

Wifey's a thick latte
with expresso curves
loves to shake when she walks
stirred talks
among hunters
who want to capture her native land
for flower beans
that'll
make man millions
stars buck from barrels
leave nebula of scattered clouds
among her mother's forest in
          Paraguay
               Brazil
                    Bolivia
covers herself with pink petals whenever Chile

her eyes a blonde roast
  brewed stares under a summer sun
    when her flavored scent of vanilla cacao
invaded nostrils
from the coast of Honduras
  enslaved
      and stripped from her Blackness
        into a caramel macchiato
shipped to the Bronx
          more potent than crack cocaine
            her caffeine leaves fiends
              wrapped around the block
                for another
hit

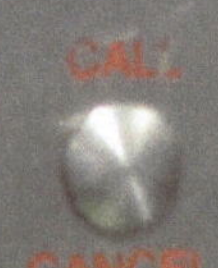

CALL
CANCEL
HOLD
NORMAL
FIREMEN SERVICE
FIRE OPERATION

20
16
12
8
4
L

21
17
13
9
5
1
18
14
10
6
2
19
15
11
7
3
DOOR OPEN
DOOR CLOSE
ALARM
EMERG STOP
PROPERTY OF N.Y.C.H.A.

Funky Joe
digging for gold

yesterday was
chicken bone
with Gata Lady's
left over

arroz con papas
bababa caboo oo oo
papa aaah
tapping concrete walls

with rusty
aluminum spoons
bababa caboo
beating metal fork gates

pulling a shopping cart
filled with empty cans
spitting rhythm
dead skin dance
on top of

pink chapped lips
shake hips
como sal y pimienta
bababa caboo oo oo

St. Mary's New Year

Black
Hispanic
male
Yankee ball cap
24 to 37 years of age
5-7 to 6 feet tall
130 to 200 lbs.
Blue denim jeans
Suspect′s on the loose
Please do not engage
Suspect is armed and
Danger   o   us
   St. Mary′s children
               Suspect Victim
          Synonymous
This will moon cycle
on-on-on-on-on-on-on
because it′s easy to kill
what looks
like
me

The first homicide of 20▮ takes place in the Bronx on Thursday morning

A 26-year-old male was fatally shot and died shortly after being rushed to Lincoln Medical Center.

48   16   SHARE THIS URL
                                           nydn.us/1B8tH4T

ADAM KAZMIERSKI/GETTY IMAGES

The first homicide of 2015 took place in the Bronx as a 26-year-old male died.

A 26-year-old Bronx man became the first city homicide of 2015 when he was fatally shot in Melrose, police said Thursday.

Herb Huntley took two bullets in the head and one in the torso in the lobby of the St. Mary's Houses on Westchester Ave. near E. 152nd St. shortly before 3 a.m., police sources said.

Emergency responders rushed Huntley to Lincoln Medical Center, but he could not be saved. He lived around the corner on Tinton Ave.

About an hour before Huntley was gunned down, two employees of the Hot Bagels deli in the Arden Heights section of Staten Island became the first gunshot victims of the new year when two men in ski masks opened fire during a botched robbery, police said.

Both victims were taken to Staten Island University North Medical Center, where they were listed in stable condition.

There were no arrests in either shooting and both incidents were under

Entry
Entry
Be the conductor
Be the traveler
But not a token

Exit
TRAIN
YOUR
THOUGHTS

TUNE INTO
YOUR
STATION

If you belive, we all will too!

I was born into the struggle.
———— Resilient by design.————

My building
Jackson A

The Story of Jerry Blood Knuckles
Part I: The Ball That Wobbled

Mothers ran with babies in their arms. Screams bounced from concrete to concrete. People got shot, but no one died. Blood painted the canvas of our street corners with rage, jealousy, and confusion. Dropping the football from my hands, I jumped behind bushes, scanning my body, whispering, "I'm not hit. I'm not. I'm good." Wiping the sweat from my brow, I got up and ran upstairs to my 13th-floor apartment.

Shoot-outs lasted about five minutes, but it felt like hours, and we talked about it for days. Cops were forced to turn around and wait for backup. John Adam's projects were right across the street from St. Mary's projects. Our neighborhoods fought with sovereign prejudice. However, the bullets never discriminated. The sweet smell of Jamaican Beef Patty wrapped in coconut bread, and redolence gun smoke, embodied our summers.

The next day, I went back outside. I noticed this strange kid in front of my building. There, by the faded wooden benches, tossing a football. He asked if I wanted to play some ball. I knew the rules, but I didn't care. I could hear the Ol' Heads in my head, "The block is hot. Be cautious of new people walking through, they're either cops or shooters from across the street."

Drugs - guns - money - and sex governed our neighborhoods, and if you possessed any influence in one of these categories, you had power.

Tossing the ball to himself, he ran for a short pass along a patch of grass slapped in the middle of St. Mary's. A sea of cement covered our projects, and brick buildings blocked the horizon. The ball flew about twenty yards when he caught it. I don't recall his name. He was a tall Puerto Rican kid with glasses and short black hair. Maybe he was setting me up?

"What's your name again?" he asked. He looked about sixteen.

"Al Boogie," I said as he walked towards me with a goofy smile.

My dad would say, "if you smile too much, many people would think you're weak. The weak do not survive very long in St. Mary's."

"We just had a shoot-out less than twenty-four hours ago.", I thought out loud.

"Try to spiral the ball like this." He said as the ball spun symmetrically perfectly in his hand.

I was athletically built at thirteen. I broke the nose of men nearly three times my age. I had been boxing since the age of nine. I knew how to jump the turnstile like a hurdler. I learned how to lose the cops running in and out of my building. I knew how to play jungle basketball. I ran like a cheetah in track meets; I came in third in the county for the 200 meters. However, I never learned to throw a football. No one ever showed me how to play football. This Puerto Rican Kid would be the first person ever to show me how to throw a ball.

"How?" I asked, staring at his hands gripping the beaten-up leather ball.

"You have to spread your fingers like this, you see. Rest your thumb right here. Then, kind of roll it off your hands like this." He tossed the ball straight into the air. Squirrels ran up and down our maple trees. Hip Hop and Salsa blasted out the project's windows. Buses were honking every few minutes, and taxi drivers were cursing out every car in its way.

It was early Saturday morning. The streets weren't as crowded, and traffic was light.

 "Yo, let me try," I said as he ran for another short pass. While gripping the ball in my hand, I saw Jerry Blood Knuckles heading in our direction.

Jerry Blood Knuckles was coming out of his building directly next to mine, on the same block. Some may say that our buildings could be like miniature cities because each of our buildings held over 500 people. Illinois, Belknap has a population of 100 people; Arizona, Oatman has 128 people; and Iowa, Saint Donatus has 135 residents. You can combine all three of these small towns, and one of our buildings will still have hundreds more living in it.

Pretending I did not see Jerry Blood Knuckles, I tossed the ball towards the six-foot Puerto Rican Kid in motion. The patch of grass was less than fifty yards long. It still wobbled as the Puerto Rican Kid caught it.

"Much better," said the Puerto Rican Kid.

"Yo Boogie hit me Sun." Jerry Blood Knuckles shouted as he entered the short-chained patch of grass we used as a football field. I tossed a wobbly pass to Jerry Blood Knuckles while looking at the Puerto Rican Kid.

Right then and there, it struck me, the Puerto Rican Kid

lacked street smarts and was unaware of the dangers that sur-rounded us. I knew who was coming in and out of the projects in all directions. I scanned half a mile easily, quickly, and seamlessly without batting an eye. That's what made you a true Bronx native, kin to St. Mary's—being able to stay on high alert while looking cool at the same time.

The Puerto Rican Kid's posture was lanky, and he pushed his glasses up to his nose every few minutes. I was about five feet, and Jerry Blood Knuckles was a few inches shorter than me. At six feet, The Puerto Rican Kid was taller than both of us. He was nothing like the project Boricuas from the city.

The Boricuas who ran parts of the city were off the chain and were nothing to be played with. One of my best friends was a Puerto Rican named Danny Boy, and he walked with the heart of ten elephants. Danny Boy looked like a choir boy; however, he was fearless. I've seen him beat down a six-foot athlete with a miniature baseball bat.

"Yo Boogie, let's play a quick game, kid," Jerry Blood Knuckles said, rolling the ball in both hands, walking towards me. He was a light-skinned Black kid. His knuckles were always scabby, and they bled sometimes. He had a habit of punching the biggest kids in their faces who did not represent St. Mary's and stomped them to the ground. He was another one that defied physics.

"Bet. I'm down for whatevah," I said in my nonchalant voice. I gave Jerry Blood Knuckles a distinct St. Mary's handshake. Hand-shakes identified what neighborhoods or crews you ran with. The wrong handshake got you beat up, robbed, or left you bleeding in the middle of the street with people walking past you minding their own business.

Plus, a handshake was a statement that you were part of a family.

"Yo, new kid, Boogie is gonna throw me the ball, and you got me on defense." Jerry Blood Knuckles ordered the Puerto Rican Kid. The Puerto Rican Kid shrugged his shoulders.

"Sure", the Puerto Rican Kid said with a smirk. This Puerto Rican Kid's problem was that he did not take anything seriously. This Puerto Rican Kid's attitude felt like we were out picking daffodils in the suburbs for the last hour. I rolled my eyes.

"Somethin' funny?" Jerry Blood Knuckles asked.

"It's whatever you want to do. I just want to play some ball", said the Puerto Rican Kid.

"Oh, I thought there was a probl'm or somethin' cuz we can scrap right here, NAH MEAN" I knew Jerry Blood Knuckles wasn't just making a threat. I grab the ball from Jerry Blood Knuckles.

"Yo fam' let's play," I said, trying to ease tensions.

Jerry Blood Knuckles was skinny and muscular. He was part of the shooting that took place yesterday. Jerry Blood Knuckles was famous for fistfights, but he was known for shooting his twenty-two. The way he stared at the Puerto Rican Kid, I sensed Jerry Blood Knuckles was interested in a different sport.

He was a white-washed Puerto Rican with no Spanish in him and spoke perfect English. He lacked the capacity to code-switch. The Puerto Rican Kid was book smart, not street smart; sometimes, people can be both, but not him. He couldn't read the energy that Jerry Blood Knuckles was displaying.

"I agree with Boogie; there's no sense to quarrel. Let's just play some ball."

"What you call'd me? a squirrel?" Jerry Blood Knuckles shouted.

"No quarrel, quarrel. No need to fight." The Puerto Rican Kid said, putting his hands to his face as Jerry Blood Knuckles steamed towards him with a crazed look in his eye.

"Yo chill b', no need to beef. Sun don't know nothin', let's play the game," I said, holding Jerry Blood Knuckles back, laughing trying to ease tensions. "Plus, I heard you had butter-fingers."

"What? I got mad skills. Please . . . you buggin'. Set it up, Boogie," Jerry Blood Knuckles responded, protecting his pride.

Jerry Blood Knuckles and I were part of the St. Mary's inner community. There were different layers and roles in this community. We protect ourselves from other crews who tried robbing or jumping us. The older guys used to rough us up, chase us down, beat us up as training to toughen us up to protect ourselves and St. Mary's.

We have been friends for years; however, since junior high school, Jerry Blood Knuckles has been hanging out with the older guys, driving fancy cars. The older guys, also known as Ol' G's, had been giving him small guns and having him smoke Angel Dust. Other times, Jerry Blood Knuckles and I were upstairs playing video games eating my mom's Honduran dishes with our crew.

I could see the fear in the Puerto Rican Kid's eyes. I learned this skill in the boxing ring. The Puerto Rican Kid's hand shook as he pushed his glasses up to his face. He no longer had a naïve look on his face. His passive attitude about St. Mary's now shifted into horror. His smile was gone. I realized that this tall sixteen-year-old had never been in a fight. This Puerto Rican had never lived in the projects or the city. He had no accent, no sense of urgency, or heightened awareness about his surroundings. He was a suburb's kid who walked into a part of the Bronx's jungle called St. Mary's projects, and one of its lions happened to smell fresh meat. Jerry Blood Knuckles gave him a cold stare with a smile that held no humor.

Jerry Blood Knuckles took off running, and I threw another wobbly ball in the air. The Puerto Rican Kid was scared to play defense as he ran alongside Jerry Blood Knuckles. The ball dropped to the ground, and Jerry Blood Knuckles pushed the Puerto Rican out his way to pick it up.
"My bad, I'mah throw it better this time b'." I said as Jerry Blood Knuckles and the Puerto Rican Kid headed towards me.

"Don't trip Boogie, let's jus' run it again b'" Jerry Blood Knuckle said with determination. The Puerto Rican Kid did not want to play anymore. He was scared and did not want to find out what would happen if he quit. The tension was thicker than pig's feet. Maybe he figured that after the game, Jerry Blood Knuckles would befriend him. The Puerto Rican Kid shot me a nervous smile. He was aware that I have been trying to help him through this ordeal. His nervous smile was a hint for me to end the game.

"Hike, hut one, hut two, hut three," I pretended to snap the ball to myself like if I were Joe Montana from the 49ers. Jerry Blood Knuckles and the Puerto Rican Kid took off. I looked in all directions. My legs pivoted forward. I threw the ball as far as I could towards Jerry Blood Knuckles. The Puerto Rican Kid had given Jerry Blood Knuckles plenty of room to catch it. It wobbled in the air, something terrible. I didn't know how to throw a ball. The ball headed towards The Puerto Rican Kid and not the wide receiver. Jerry Blood Knuckles jumped on the Puerto Rican Kid to catch the ball. They both fell. The Puerto Rican landed on Jerry Blood Knuckles. The Puerto Rican Kid was easily fifty pounds heavier than Jerry Blood Knuckles. The Puerto Rican rolled off of him like he was a house cat. They both jumped to their feet.

"I'm sorry, man. I'm so sorry. I didn't mea . . ." Jerry Blood Knuckles punched the Puerto Rican Kid right in his mouth before he could finish apologizing. The Puerto Rican Kid threw his hands towards his face trying to cover himself. It was like watching a Mike Tyson Punch-Out video game. The Puerto Rican Kid was physically more prominent than Jerry Blood Knuckles. The laws of physics can never compete with pure will. It does not matter how many muscles, how tall, or much you weigh when you fight with a person from the Bronx. Size is irrelevant. It's all about guts, heart, and fearlessness. Whoever is willing to go beyond the extreme of savagery usually wins—the sport of survival.

"Stop, please. Someone help."

Jerry Blood Knuckles just kept throwing a cluster of punches. His knuckles were connecting to the Puerto Rican's chin, nose, and forehead. The Puerto Rican Kid fell on his back pleading. I stood watching. I had to let Jerry Blood Knuckles finish him off. The Puerto Rican Kid was friendly, but Jerry Blood Knuckles needed to make him an example. I wasn't about to pick a side, but in retrospect, I did. "Boogie, help me, please." I shook my head and gave the Puerto Rican Kid a cold stare. I wasn't about to take the side of a stranger over someone from St. Mary's. I had to live in St. Mary's. Jerry Blood Knuckles sat on top of him and swung his closed fist in all directions.

"This is St. Mary's, punk. Nobody messes with St. Mary's." Knuckles and elbows were flying towards the Puerto Rican Kid's head. When Jerry Blood Knuckles was getting tired, he got up and started kicking him. I saw a six-foot giant crying into a fetal position lying on a patch of grass. His glasses were broken. Blood was running from his nose. Although I was horrified by Jerry Blood Knuckles' explosion, I had to pretend like I was getting bored. I couldn't display any sign of weakness.

"Yo b', this is whack. Let's go upstairs and play some video games," I said, walking towards Jerry Blood Knuckles. If I had shown any excitement, it would have just pumped him up even more. He threw his last few kicks.

"Don't evah let me catch you in St. Mary's," he yelled into the Puerto Rican Kid's face that was still lying on the floor shaking. Jerry Blood Knuckles picked up the ball.
"Let's go, Boogie. I got the first controller."

"Oh hell nah . . . I won the last game."

Jerry Blood Knuckles switched from rage to laughing about why he should have brought his controller from his apartment. Jerry Blood Knuckles and I went upstairs as if the fight never took place.

We left the Puerto Rican Kid there sobbing—the guilt rummage through my stomach. I knew the rules. I should have told the Puerto Rican Kid that I wasn't interested in a game. I should've played by myself. I should have stayed upstairs and let the suburb kid realize that no one was coming out to play that day. We had a shoot-out the day before. I was warned. St. Mary's was at war, and Jerry Blood Knuckles was one of her soldiers. Jerry Blood Knuckles wasn't coming outside to play ball. I knew that the moment he stepped out of his building, he would investigate who the new kid was. I could've stopped the game then, but I wanted to play. I wanted to learn how to throw a straight ball. Even now, when I throw a football, it still wobbles.

Strum

SHE SERENADES THE BEAST WITH MELODIC STREET PERCUSSIONS
YOU CAN HEAR HER SONG WHEN SHE HUMS
HER VOCALS STRUM
DECIBELS THAT LEAVE YOUR EARDRUMS IN CONCUSSION

AP
vila
roduction
Avila PRODUCTION

B4MooN
Screenplay

By
Alex Avila

FADE IN:
EXT. Flashing light opening with B4Moon:

FADE IN:

EXT. Cracked cement wall in the backdrop, an IMMIGRANT
BIRD in route, and a WITNESS tells its story.

WITNESS
Immigrant Bird
flew passed 3rd
avenue
yellow cabs screaming'
at red lights
Boonk Boonk Boonk Boooank
Left wing reopened wound
3 nights ago from Mexico
by barbed wire borders biting
tearing feathers
feathers broken
bleeding down
iron   stainless steel train
both   headed towards
 St. Mary's project
now
its blood drip baptizing ground
painting the leaves on its way
to St. Mary's red
Feathers grey like the
streets
scattered glass

FADE IN:

EXT. We see St. Mary's projects and an IMMIGRANT BIRD try-ing to get there. WITNESS stares at the IMMIGRANT BIRD.

> WITNESS
> gummy cement concrete
> bottom beak slightly cracked
> from running into a Macy's building
> on 34th street

FADE IN:

EXT. A clear night sky building's blowing smoke in the air. WIT-NESS reflects the IMMIGRANT BIRD's travel and wonders if it will make it to St. Mary's.

> WITNESS
> the night before
> coyotes try to steal its wings
> to sell in the black-market
> lights out gleamed
> the dippers and the North Star

FADE IN:

EXT. St. Mary's comes closer into view for the IMMIGRANT BIRD. The sun is starting to disappear. The WITNESS is in awe.

> WITNESS
> Immigrant Bird's convinced
> Buildings eat trees
> and grow like square rocks
> statues

                              monuments   covered with
glass eyes

                              flying up Westchester Ave
                              Glancing at barbed wires
                               surrounding walls
                               of a juvenile hall
                              across the street from children
                              going to school
                               chain-gang digging through walls
                              with toothbrushes
                              hiding books under bunk
                              beds six by four walls
                              Immigrant Bird's
                              Bleeding towards St. Mary's

FADE IN:

EXT. The WITNESS sees the IMMIGRANT BIRD make it to St.
Mary's before sun down.

                              WITNESS
                              Immigrant Bird crash
                              landing on the top of
                              the 21st floor of building
                               number 645
                              nursing a strained right foot
                              limping hopping limping hopping
                               limping
                              on pebbled rocks
                              undisturbed by the shootings sirens
                              trains click clacking along the tracks
                              bleeding limping hopping
                              towards a chimney
                              smoking up to a falling sun

Day 2

smitty smacks
drags
bum left foot
under
jackson ave tracks
iron
drip spit piss coke
steel
oil face caked
stuck
in st. mary's project

Paper Poet
Screenplay

By
Alex Avila

FADE IN:
EXT. Water drops Paper Poet

EXT. Morning sun over the Silhouette Mountains of Forest Falls.
THE POET.

THE POET (voice)
I heard a Poet
left the Bronx
with a pen
bleeding off the margins
on a pad   period
disintegrating through project walls
passing   Bobby's Bodegas
Bx Bus Stops
Uterus – corner blocks

FADE IN:

EXT. THE POET sketched himself walking through the forest.

THE POET (voice)
used train tunnels like fallopian
 tubes
his mind is one in millions of eggs
looking to be broken into
wanting to birth ideas
ideas that run wild
shuffling
shuffling
shuffling
shuffling   through wilderness
through virgin leaves
through un-molested flower beds

                              pages in search of their biological
                              mother
mothers whose limbs are chopped
to build homes boats bridges

EXT. THE POET writes poetry on a big rock.

                              THE POET (voice)
                              mothers who smoke smog like meth
pipes
                              mothers who are ripped from their
roots and   sold to traffickers
                              you can find her at Home-depot
worth less than   minimum
wage
                              her children handcuffed looking for
                              work

EXT. THE POET whispers to redwood trees.

                              THE POET (voice)
                              la migra   la migra
                              la migra

FADE IN:

EXT. THE POET moves through the wilderness.

                              THE POET (voice)
                              in search of purpose
                              through pen and paper
                              bleeding
                              shuffling
                              bleeding

                    shuffling
                    shuffling
                    shuffling   through pages

                    pages that sketched bodies on
                    St. Mary's
                    side   walks
                    bodies that lay for hours

EXT. THE POET watches the leaves and branches fall.

                         THE POET's (voice)
                         flies hovering
                         ambulance stuck in traffic
                         move back – move back
                         there's nothing here to see
                         they said
                         A Poet
                         wanting to paint the
                    Statue of Liberty black
                              brown bronze
                         anything that reflect the migrants of
                         today.
                         A Poet and his Papers

FADE IN:

EXT. THE POET's painting the forest with words.

                         THE POET (voice)
                         wanting to breastfeed peace between
                         bloods crips latin kings queens Israel
                         Palestine
                         shh shh shhhhh   hoping to

stop the crying

> A Poet and his Papers
> shuffling
> shuffling
> shuffling   through pages
> nursing them with words of
> encouragement
> Brilliant
> Even when you forget your name
> and no longer
> know the road back

FADE IN:

EXT. THE POET resurrects words from trees to paper.

> THE POET (voice)
>> Beautiful
>> Even when your hair knots rust
>> under sun bright
>> even when you've gone days without
>> brushing
>> your teeth
>> weeks without bathing
>> white shirt dims
>> resilient

EXT. THE POET's on the run from words that inflame hatred.

> THE POET (voice)
>> even after the sixth eviction

> A Poet and Paper
> married in struggle

On a journey for truth

Ducking dodging
Inflamed words

EXT. THE POET adjusts on a big rock.

> THE POET (voice)
> looking to cremate ideas before they
> crawl

FADE IN:

EXT. THE POET's by the red tree ducking and running the de-
struction of man, shuffling through his pages.

> THE POET (voice)
> A Poet and his Paper
> Shuffling
> Shuffling
> Shuffling   through wilderness

THAT NIGHT
we met over a dog bite

ST. Mary's Shah
Sreenplay

By
Alex Avila

  Characters
THE WITNESS
THE PREACER
WILLIE (the vet)
FREDDY FOX (friend of the vet)
THE POET

     EXT. Opening with exploding inks. From a
     moving train as the voice of THE POET
speaks.

                         THE POET (voice)
                         St. Mary's
                         She-shah-she-shah
                         She shall overcome
                         War drums
                         bullet echo eardrums
                         bulla blaah blackah blackah
blackah
                         night songs
                         sir(+o)n
                         her to cook
                         rock brick black brown
                         swing sound
                         che rry ooo
                         blow snow
                         up nose
                         winters minds

     EXT.The Preacher is under ST.MARY'S PROJ-
ECT'S train station in a moving car, the voice
of THE POET speaks.

                         THE POET (voice)
                         Spring Preacher blind
                         walked pass Jesus

on a the 2 train
asking for change
Mira Negro, can you help a
brother out, a burger or
so-m'hmm
Spring Preacher ignored him
buried his nose in the bible
because the man smelled like
vomit
eyes bloodshot red like a
fallen comet
nappy hair of wool
skin of bronze
getting off in The Bronx
of St. Mary's Projects
Next Stop Jackson Avenue

EXT. Snow dust flying all around and THE POET.

THE POET (voice)
She-shah-she-shah
She shall overcome
St. Mary's children
run
Duck - Duck - Duck Grey Goose
bottles
thrown from 21 stories
where books serve sentences
like candy for parents
to eat 25 to life
behind barred windows

EXT. Willie, the vet, comes up slow in his
military uniform with no gun. He looks slowly
to both sides. He can't tell the difference
between St. Mary's projects and Iraq.

184

                    THE POET (voice)
                    shell shock vet
                    thinks St. Mary's is Iraq,
                    Afghanistan, Pakistan

EXT. FREDDY FOX pleading with WILLIE.

                    FREDDY FOX (voice)
                    yo man   chill man
                    put the gun down
                    Willie it's me
                    Freddy Fox from up the block
                    It's me Freddy

                    WILLIE (voice)
                    Lay low Fred
                    You hear'em Fred
                    You hear'em
                    They tryin' to kill us Fred
                    Like they did Bill, Craig,
                    Smith
                    Fred Lay low
                    Sweat che rry   ooo
                    We gonna shootem
                    And go on home
                    Stay low
                    Sweat che rry   ooo
                    We gonna burry'em
                    And go on home

FREE GLASSES
If you can't afford to change the lens
switch perspectives.
New angle.
New day.
MARCH 34, 2040 10AM TO 4PM
ANY OPEN GROUNDS, ANY CITY

When I open
my door

The Story of Diesel
Part I: The Junior High Fight That Built A Bond

Diesel and I became close friends over a fight in middle school many years ago. We have known each other growing up since elementary school but never spoke until the fight in junior high school. What led up to the dispute was unclear.

"Yo sun, you think you could just walk through here like it's sweet," yelled Mo' from across the hall. I.S. 162 held about a few hundred students. Mo' was the biggest, toughest, muscular kid in middle school, and everyone moved out his way when he walked the halls.

"I can walk where I want. It's a free country." Diesel said casually, without batting an eye.

Our school was attended by all the kids from the projects in the surrounding neighborhoods. This form of diversity would have been a beautiful experiment, but this was during the Crack-Cocaine era, which turned our communities into war zones. Each project was like its own country protected by crews, no different than tribes, the military, or political parties fighting over real estate.

"Let's see what happens when I punch you in the mouth." Mo' screamed, rushing towards Diesel. The hall was crowded with seventh and eighth-graders. Most of the teachers were afraid of the students, and the one security guard we had was flaky at best.

Mo' slammed Diesel into the hall lockers. I swiftly pushed my arms between Diesel and Mo' to separate them both. Students caused traffic trying to capture what was happening. Their growing presence spewed gas onto the scene, and Mo' was a walking match.

"Yo fam, it's not that serious. Let's just go to class and chill out." I said, to Mo' and Diesel, trying to calm everyone down. Normally, I mind business and keep to myself, but Diesel was from St. Mary's, and I couldn't let these two go at it with good consciousness. Everyone was aware that Mo's older brothers were well-known drug dealers from the John Adams Project. The last thing anyone needed was problems with his family.

"You need to get out of my face and mind your business." Mo' spat back. The second floor got loud with Oohs and Aahs.

Mo' swung his right fist towards my head. I ducked, moving my body under his wild swing. I ended up behind him. With the momentum of his first punch, I pushed him, and he crashed into the lockers. What seemed like minutes felt like hours. Diesel was skinny and tall. Diesel and I looked at each other, understanding there was no turning back from this moment.

"I'm down for whatevah you want to do Mo' ain't nobody scared of you." Diesel spat, with his chest out while gripping his knuckles.

"Mo', bro, that was an accident. I don't want any problems, fam. D' and I are just goin' to . . ." I said, hoping for one glimmer of opportunity to stop the situation from exploding. However, the fuel was lit, and I was right in its path.

Mo's skin was dark chocolate with no scratches. He always took his shirt off during gym class to flex. Everyone has seen Mo' punching someone in the face countless times, either in the boys' locker room, lunchtime, or after school. A Mo' incident ended with someone screaming, bleeding, and humiliated. People heard of me fighting and knocking down grown men, but none of these students ever saw it. Mo' believed since I was trying to stop the fight that I was scared, on the contrary. I grew up getting beat down in elementary school all the time; black eyes, bruises and had my head cracked open, which required stitches. Fighting was a way of life in the Bronx, especially coming from St. Mary's. My father was tired of the beatdowns and enrolled me into a professional gym called Jerome's Boxing Gym. Infested with savages, this was the grittiest, dirtiest facility one would ever encounter in the Bronx, and I loved it. Before Jerome's Boxing Gym, I lost every fight.

"Bet." Mo' said to the lockers. Everyone knew what that one word signified. When he turned around, his face was dark purple. He pushed himself off the lockers and started swinging. Jerome's Boxing Gym taught me plenty. One of those lessons was never starting a fight, but you must know how to finish it.

When I entered Jerome's Boxing Gym, I was a skinny-bird-chest-loud-mouth kid who was tired of getting bullied. The trainers stayed away from little kids like myself because we were hard to train. I recall one of the older fighters talking with the Olympic champion Coach Gomez, saying that I talked a lot of trash for someone that was always getting knocked down to the canvas. Coach Gomez's response was, "You can always teach skills, but you can't teach heart. The kid has heart and gets up every time." Coach Gomez took me in. He showed me how to street fight, box, and combine the two in and out of the ring, which changed my life. I stopped talking trash, and I lost my wild, nervous energy. I was calm under pressure and strategic. A person's size was irrelevant. Heart, creativity, strategy, patients, and speed were everything. By the time I was thirteen, I was undefeated in all my weight classes. I was sparring grown men, sometimes knocking them down but learning to outmaneuver their ferociousness in the ring, most of the time. To everyone else at school, Mo' was Hercules. To me, Mo' was a big baby seeking attention that he probably did not get at home.

I was able to move my head and shift my weight out of Mo's way. What happened next was a combination of luck, coincidence, excellent positioning, and perfect timing.

Time did slow down significantly. The noise from the other students yelling became incoherent, like background noise underwater. Mo' and I were the same height. He looked physically dominant with an extra 30 pounds of muscle. His fist was inches from my face. Without disrupting his motion, I grabbed his right hand, placing it over my shoulder. His chest landed on my back, and I bent my knees to lift him. I felt his entire weight on my back and, with the push of my knees, threw him into the nearest trash can a few feet away. Mo' fell headfirst, and the hallway exploded. Students were jumping and shouting. Diesel froze with disbelief. I was controlling my breathing, ready for Mo's next wild swing.

Mo' jumped out of the trash can onto his feet. Although he was gripping his fist, wiping apple juice off his face, his eyes said everything. Fighters and boxers know that the eyes always give it away. He was scared and embarrassed. I was in a fighting stance, ready for whatever came next. I got tackled by security and the dean. I was so focused on Mo', I never saw the tackle coming. My face was shoved to the floor with the security's knees on my back. I never took my eyes off of Mo'. His face was soaking with reality, and the truth was that I was the first person at school to blow out his fuse. Subconsciously, Mo' and I knew the fight was over when he got up from the trash can. His steam was gone, and his tough-guy image, to me at least, vanished the moment we locked eyes. There's no telling what would have happened if I had another fifteen seconds; however, Mo' and I both knew he was not going to survive. I went from being this

bummy, extra big clothes, bowl-hair-cut, awkward-looking kid to be-
coming popular over one moment. No one talked or hung out with
me before that moment. Diesel, one of the best-dressed kids that
half the girls went crazy over at school, was now shouting my name.

"That's my boy, that's my boy right there. St. Mary's baby." Diesel
shouted, pointing in my direction. A person from the outside would
have thought Diesel and I were brothers. He talked about me like we
were friends all our lives.

In the dean's office, the circumstances were interesting. The dean did
not care about suspending us. "Look, I need to know if we can end
this right here in my office, right now. The last thing I need is the
neighborhood bringing their war to the front of my doorstep. I won't
call your parents. Hell, there won't even be an incident report if you
two could squash your problems now." The dean pleaded. Mo' and I
sat silently, and we looked over at one another.

"There isn't going to be a problem from me. I'm cool if you are
cool? I won't say another word about today." I said, looking over
at Mo'. He nodded in agreement, and the dean forced us to shake
hands.

I kept my word and never talked about the incident. Mo's
older brothers never showed up to the school to terrorize Diesel and
me. I became popular overnight. I went from this awkward-bum-
my-loner kid with a bowl-cut to girls asking me out on dates and the
guys walking me to Jerome's Boxing Gym after school. It was impos-
sible to keep the incident under wraps, especially with Diesel.

"Ey-yo, I know you know my boy's quick with his hands. He body-
slammed Mo' and dropped kicked him into the trash bin, last week?"

192

said Diesel to a table full of girls at lunchtime. He was different from what I expected. I thought he would be reserved about the matter, and he was quite the opposite. Diesel told anyone who would listen about the fight. The story changed every week. By the end of the year, I overheard that I slammed Mo's face on several lockers, picking him up by his throat and throwing him fifteen feet into the trash bin with one hand.

Por Favor

no pares la musicaaaaaaaa
Sha-lalasha-lalalala

Tito smacking elephant skin
younger brother
trying to pace
with the salsa
seasoning through the radio

Tonia's butter baking plantains
Shake   shake   shake brown sugar

Ol' man picking boogers
tellin' stories
how a carton of milk
use to cost 2 Kennedy coins
not no damn $4
Creo que es mas major en Honduras
No entiendo hombre!
As he flicks the dried specimen on the grey tiled floor
watching Univison

Carla puts her hands to her breast
to feed a newborn who hollers
in a kitchen hotter
 than hands pickin' summer's cotton
green onions sizzle dance in scarred pans
peeling with Teflon   metal   rust
a college student wrinkles his face in distrust
Tonia says
It's to add flavor mijo   no te hagas
Onions chop   chopped   and chopping
Miguel   Tonia yells   over Tito's banging drum

todavia no has terminado con el eshopping
¿dónde está la sal?

Lalala   shalalala lala

Por favor   Mama   hold the bacon
                                              Says the college student
                                               Tito stopped smackin' skin
                                     Ol' man finger stuck to his nose as he froze
                                        Nipple popped out of the newborn's gums
                                     Miguel drops the shopping bags on the floor
                                               from his second trip to the store
                                              Tonia's tong gripping pork's tongue
                                               stared stung into her baby's eyes
                                                             wondering
                                                                 who
stole her   son's song

La   la   laaaaa

Story of Diesel
Part II: The Robbery

His mother raised him, and none of us ever inquired about his dad. At a young age, he had to be the man of the house while his mother went to college. She eventually got a job working for a law firm. She left her Saint Mary's apartment with Diesel when she bought a house in Connecticut. The conditions were that Diesel maintains the apartment's monthly payments or moves in with his mother in Connecticut. She paid the apartment seven months in advance to give Diesel time to find work. Diesel did not want to go to college; he wanted to stay in St. Mary's to prove that he could be his own man. He did well for about a year, but he started to steer in a different direction after that.

"Yo Boogz, I found this joint up in Parkchester, and it's an easy lick."

"Diesel, what you talkin' 'bout bro. You' bugging." I said, laughing him off.

"I'm serious, Boogz. This is the one. It's nowhere near the hood. It's these uppity Black folks who are barely home, and I got their schedule from my boy Rock."

"Schedule? Are you serious? Rock? How long you've been plotting this?" I said, scratching my face, as we sat on the St. Mary's wood benches in front of Diesel's building.

"Boogz, you're in or what? I don't need a lecture, yo. I ran this plan through my head for six months. This is going to work b'." He said with conviction. Sunday nights always had a sense of calmness, especially in the summer.

"You dead serious? I thought you were feeling your new job. Did you get fired or somethin'?." I said, looking suspicious

"I know you ain't scared. We from St. Mary's baby, The Boogie Down Bronx, since when you start getting soft. Plus, there's possibly $50,000 we can cut you in on."

"When you thinkin' about doing this?" I asked reluctantly.

"Next Saturday. Here's the address and the times to scope it out if you wanted to roll through before the jump." He said, tossing a wrinkled folded piece of paper with an address and a long list of documented dates and times they have visited the place.

The next day, I took the bus, which was only twenty minutes. The place was nice. A three-story house. A quiet neighborhood with expensive cars parked on each corner. People were walking their dogs and coming home from work. There were no alcoholics or drug addicts anywhere. The street was spotless compared to Saint Mary's.

The following day, I took the train, which took about thirty minutes because I had to take two different trains. Every time I went back to check this place out, I felt poorer and poorer. The resentment started building up, and the embarrassment began to cloud my head. We have seen places like this on TV growing up. It was easier to watch on tv than in person; it just made my stomach hurt and my chest cave. I saw why Diesel wanted to rob these people. These people walked without a care in the world, and we had to watch every step we took or else face the consequences in St. Mary's. There were no screams, people fighting, arguments, sirens from ambulances racing down the street, police patrols, or shootouts. It was not about the money; it was about robbing these people of their naivety and privilege. I picked up the payphone to call Diesel and said, "I'm in."

On the day of the robbery, Diesel changed the break-in time from 11:30 am to 3:30 pm. It was true that the elderly Black couple was not home during the times he suggested; however, it was a horrible idea because that was when the elementary kids got out of school, rush hour.

"Yo, what's your problem? Why would you do something stupid like that? I'm already over here." I screamed on the payphone. I was several blocks away when I received his page on my hip—the night before, we agreed to go separately and meet up at the house simultaneously.

"Listen, Boogz, trust me, we good. This way, we can blend in with the crowd before rush hour." I hung up the phone. I rushed quarters into the payphone and called up B-Suave, asking him if he wanted to play some basketball.

B-Sauve and I grew up in St. Mary's. Fights, shootouts, block parties, the birth of hip-hop, and people jumping off the 21st floor; we saw it all. We were brothers birthed by different mothers. We dressed alike, laughed at the most inappropriate moments, and fought side by side against anyone curious enough to test us.

At 5' 10, I tried dunking the ball on B-Sauve, but he smacked it right out of my hand. He was about 6' 2, light-skinned, with naturally wavy hair. We look like total opposites next to each other, night and day. However, we thought like one body whenever it came to girls, sports, and danger. We moved like twins. I did not tell Suave about Diesel's proposal because it felt rushed, and he would have talked me out of it. In my mind, I figured, I would share the money with him after and tell him all about it. It was 5 pm, and my pager did not go off. "Maybe Diesel called it off." I thought.

"You good, Boogz? You seemed distracted."

"Naw, it's nothin'. Run it back." I said, feeling the pressure alleviating from my head.

The following day, the neighborhood was talking about Diesel and Rock getting locked up. It felt like someone stepped on my chest and stopped the oxygen from going to my head.

Some said that he was caught leaving the apartment with goods in his hands, that a cop just happened to be walking by while they were walking out. Others say that one of the residents called the cops on suspicion of thugs surveying their neighborhoods for weeks. One even claimed that the husband came home early and that an altercation turned physical that ultimately led to their arrest. Either way, they were sent to Rikers Island, and no one knew when they were coming back to St. Mary's. My eyes were filled with guilt, and my mouth was dry with embarrassment. Looking out my window, I thought, "I let Diesel down. If I had been there, the situation would have been different." The phone rings.

"This is the operator. Do you accept a call from Rikers Island? This call would be charged . . ."

"Yes, yes, I accept the charges," I said.

"Hold on while we connect your call."

"Is this Boogz?"

"Yo, who's this?" I said, perplexed with the stranger on the other line.

"We know where you live. You're gonna die. We are going to kill you."

"You know where I'm at, St. Mary's baby! You feelin' tough come by anytime, playboy. Ain't nobody scared over here." The stranger hung up. I received calls like this monthly for almost a year.

Story of Diesel
Part III: B-Suave: The Punch that Saved My Life

We hopped the train on Jackson Avenue, timing the arrival of the 2 Train.

"Sun, I haven't seen Diesel in two years," I said with excitement.

"I don't know, Boogz, something sounded off about the invite over the phone. I mean, that's my guy too but. . ." B-Sauve paused, staring out the window as the train was blanketed with darkness under the tunnel.

"He's solid. Rikers didn't change him. He's from St. Mary's. Diesel's one of us." I exclaimed.

"Next stop, Grand Central Station. Please stand clear for closing doors.", sounded over the loudspeakers.

I was excited about seeing Diesel at his new home in Jersey. He moved in with his dad after he got out of jail. However, I never told B-Sauve exactly how Diesel went to jail. The afternoon of the robbery, I was supposed to be there.

The train swayed side to side. B-Sauve and I never took the train to Jersey. We usually rode in someone's car, and this was our first time. For New Yorkers, riding the train was as easy as walking. Put us anywhere in the world with a transit system, and we will figure it out over a slice of pizza.

"Yo B' I hope he has food at his crib. I'm starving."
"It's a house party. Of course, there's food, plus we're spending the night. We were on the last train going or coming from Jersey tonight. We could raid his fridge." I said jokingly.

"Aight! That's your mans, though, so he better come correct."
B-Suave stressed, holding his stomach. Looking out the window,
Jersey had more trees and greenery than St. Mary's. We were passing
two-story houses with front yards and backyards.

B-Sauve and I got off the platform and waited outside the
train station for Diesel to pick us up. If it were not for the station,
we would have been standing around in complete darkness. New
York City has tall buildings that lit up the streets. Here, the houses
were space out towered by trees. The crickets dominated the night
with their music. He pulled to the station playing the LOX from Ruff
Ryders in an old boxy Honda Civic.

"What's good family. I missed ya'll. Boogz still looks the same. Damn
B-Suave, what you grew another couple inches? Pause. Yo' we gotta
go, the crib's getting crowded." Diesel said, hugging the both of us
and walking back towards his car. "Pop's outta town for another four
days, and I got the crib to myself. Yo Boogz, we gotta catch up, fam."

"No doubt! You my guy. So what's Jersey like?" I said, looking out his
father's car's foggy windows.

"It's real, nah mean. Don't let these trees fool you. They got their
parts where you gotta be on your p's and q's. It's no St. Mary's. For
the most part, it's chill where my dad stays." Diesel said as he turned
the corner going towards this two-story colonial house. The music
was loud enough to hear for at least a few blocks. All the other hous-
es were quiet.

"This is the crib, fellas. Mi casa su casa. Let me introduce some of
my people real quick." Diesel said as he jumped out of the car. He
moved like a celebrity through the crowd, shaking hands, giving
hugs, and using a term from New York - giving dap. "This is Brolic,
202

Get Cash, Lolo, Freezer . . ." He introduced us for another twenty minutes as he worked the audience. Most of the girls were social, but the guys gave B-Suave and me a look of disdain. About twenty or thirty guys had on Timberland boots, Nikes, fitted caps, and Durags. Alcohol and weed smoke was everywhere.

"Yo Diesel, what's up with your boys. They're looking at us kinda of funny." B-Suave said, surveying the room.

"Don't worry about them; they need to loosen up. It's all good." Diesel said.
"What's good Queen, it's a beautiful night, right?" I said in my Bronx swagger.

"Yo, you can't call any of these girls Queen," Brolic said, with a bit of extra-base in his voice. He was over six feet with a 220-pound physique.

"I can say whatevah I want. It's a free county." I said, looking up at him with a smirk.

"Yo Boogz, Brolic . . . chill-out. There's a lot of girls, nah mean. Let's have some fun." Diesel said with the biggest smile, which broke the tension immediately.

B-Suave gave me a St. Mary's look that read we needed to prepare for whatever the night may bring. Diesel was in a zone. B-Suave and I felt out of place. There was no warmth in the room. We took the last train to get here. B-Suave and I believed there were guns and knives tucked under some of the apparel worn in the room.

"Yo Boogz, I don't know what this is, but I lost my appetite. Keep your eyes open. It's just us, and your boy's gone Hollywood." B-Suave said, pointing at Diesel, who was enjoying being the life of the party.

"We're from St. Mary's. I am down for whatevah the night brings." I said, balling both fists in my pants pockets.

The music was loud. Wu-Tang Clan bounced from wall to wall. Some people danced, but many stood hanging by the walls talking and looking around. The walls looked like a cream color. It was hard to look at the pictures or furniture with everyone standing around or sitting down. It felt like it was a nice house, but then again, I grew up in the projects my whole life. I could not tell you how a nice or decent place was supposed to look.

Diesel found his way back to B-Sauve and I. "Yo Boogz, B-Suave, I gotta go pick someone else up. I'll be back. You should be good. Make yourself at home." Diesel said, smiling the entire time.

"What?" I said, bewildered by the statement.

"Don't trip. You're my guest. No one is going to mess with you'. I'll be back." And like that, Diesel left us. Ten minutes later, someone stopped the music.

"Alright! Nobody is leaving without paying up. You're gonna empty out your pockets and pay us to leave." Brolic said, locking the front door while Lolo closed the back doors. The room went quiet. No one knew whether this was a joke or a setup. Get Cash stood by the doorway. Brolic and Freezer moved in unison to their first victim. He was about my height, a skinny Black kid with curls. "Cough up the cash sun," Brolic said while slamming the young man, shaking the picture frames off of the walls. My eyes could not believe it. Brolic and Freezer were emptying pockets and purses and people candidly just gave up their money and jewelry. My jaws dropped with disbelief,

and B-Suave was stunned with disappointment. They worked half
the room and still did not let anyone leave. Brolic and Freezer headed
towards B-Suave and me.

Brolic towered over me with this grimacing look on his
face. Sweat was coming down his forehead. My chest was pound-
ing, and the body's in the room went motionless. From the moment
we walked through Diesel's doors, there was tension surrounding
B-Suave and me.

"You know what it is, run it." Brolic spat in my face.
"I'm from St. Mary's. I'm not giving you anything. You gotta kill me."
I yelled in his face. I did not plan to say those words. A more vital
spirit possessed me. I was like a fully charged battery pack. I did not
have to look at B-Suave's face to know that I possibly signed our
death certificate at that moment. We were in another state by our-
selves, with no weapons of our own, not even a pencil. Brolic had at
least fifteen guys from his crew at this party.

"What? Are you crazy? Yo Hoffa, take my shirt." Brolic said, remov-
ing his shirt rapidly. B-Suave and I were standing by the stairwell that
led to the bedroom upstairs. Brolic had thick gorilla hands lunging
towards my neck. He was quick, and I did not anticipate his action.
Before I could move, his hands were around my neck with his entire
body's weight. My head banged the wall. B-Suave punched Brolic
in the face and swung him off me while ducking Freezer's lightning
punch. My fist crashed into someone's face running in my direction.
B-Suave and I were punching people left and right. We stood back
to back, and you could hear our fists cracking against skulls jump-
ing towards us. We moved in a circular motion, landing in the living
room. Intuitively we got closer to the wall reducing the chances of
getting tackled by Brolic's crew members. We were running high on
adrenaline. There was blood spilling, screaming, crying, and yelling

happening all at once. St. Marys had been teaching us to fight our whole lives, and now here we were. "Stop being punks and get them," Brolic yelled behind his crew. They looked beaten, scared, and embarrassed—two against fifteen.

In my mind, it was only a matter of time before someone grabbed a gun or knife. We were too strong, quick, desperate, and ferocious with every blow we threw. We were fighting for our lives. They kept getting up from the floor and falling back into their half a moon formation. I had to buy us some time. Diesel had to be close by and should be back here any second, I thought. I needed to do something dramatic and unpredictable, or we were going to die.

"You know what. Everybody's dead. I'm going upstairs to get my gun, and I am letting loose on everybody. People were trampling over each other, stepping on each other's chest and hands, trying to rush the door at the same time. B-Suave and I ran upstairs to the nearest bedroom. We were panting, sweating, and dropping to the bedroom floor.

"Boogz, you killed us. Why would you say that? Why? What if they come upstairs with real guns? We don't have any guns." B-Suave yelled at me from across the room.
"I know. I know. I messed up. I . . . My bad. I just . . . I . . ." I did not have a real response. B-Suave was right.

My neck started burning, and I realized my neck was bleeding from Brolic choking me earlier. The back of my head felt sore and had a knot. My hands felt swollen, my knuckles bruised. Our faces did not have a single scratch. Our clothes were torn and ripped. Out of the entire night, B-Suave was not upset that I stood up to Brolic or that we fought a whole crew by ourselves. He was angry that I lied about a gun. B-Suave was my brother who was willing to die for morals, integrity, and principles but not for a lie. B-Suave was the real hero of the night. Things were slowing down.

"What happened? My house . . . Who did this? Boogz. I'll bet you this was Boogz. Boogz is always in some mess." Diesel returned screaming and kicking everyone out. Cars were driving off fast. There was a glimmer of hope. Maybe we still had a chance to see St. Mary's again.

We stood up all night because we could not sleep. Diesel assured us that we were safe, but we did not trust it. We started laughing once we got on the train station's platform that morning, heading back to New York, more importantly, St. Mary's. We were on high alert until the train started moving. We stared out the window with deep reflection. We were lost in our thoughts for a few minutes, then B-Suave turned, facing me with disgust.

"Why did Diesel set us up last night to get jumped and robbed? He never went to pick anyone up. We got off the last train coming to Jersey. He left us there as bait, knowing the only person we knew was him. Why?"

The thought never crossed my mind. B-Suave read all the signs. I was blinded by loyalty, old memories of a past friendship and kinship birthed from St. Mary's. Now my real brother and kin, B-Suave, was asking questions. The threats from Rikers Island all started to make sense. Diesel had it in for me, and he saw me as his enemy.

"I was supposed to be there the afternoon of the robbery, the day Diesel and Rock went to jail."

Daddy's
girl
Avila PRODUCTION

Indigenous

Abuelo

The Story of Jerry Blood Knuckles
Part II: Mr. Gary

My hands rushed to the bathroom, locking the door behind me. It was Saturday, and school was out. Becky Brown From The Boogie Down was sure to be downstairs hanging with her friends on the wooden tagged benches. The Potpourri air freshener left a slight sting on my armpits and chest. This routine was a change from my usual Baking Soda, Old Spice, and Musk deodorant; puberty had a funny way of producing extra sweat. I was not going to let that stop me from trying to ask Becky Brown out on a date. Every year, I freeze, stutter, change the subject, fumble the words that I genuinely want to tell her, but I have been practicing all summer, and today it will be a reality. St. Mary's throwing a Hip Hop block party today, and that's where I will make my move.

The armpits of my undershirt look like I had a bag of lemons in a headlock. The tub was dripping with watered pinks, oranges, and blues from the rack of clothes drying above it. I grabbed my slightly damped Batman underwear from the hanger next to my brother's wet socks – I was the oldest of six boys. With my index finger, I brushed my somewhat visible mustache while holding my crotch, saying, "YO SHORTIE . . . Yo shortie . . . Yooo shortie.", taking the base out of my voice and shaking my head with disapproval in the mirror. "Nah yo, I gotta be original b'." I mumbled, running a black plastic afro pick through my nappy head. "Yo Ma, what's wrong wit' your boy-friend leaving you out here for these thirst-buckets to come harass you." I said, not impressed with myself. It was too corny.

A few days ago, Becky Brown From The Boogie Down and I were in the same elevator for a hot minute after school. Okay, maybe around thirty seconds. Her strawberry waxed lipstick overpowered the oily musty-pissy-beer steel-smelling elevator. She was about half a foot shorter than me, and her black flat-ironed hair went past her shoulders gracefully. She wasn't like the other girls. She took pride in her presentation. The other Black girls in my building barbecued their hairpieces with hot combs leaving it brittle, choppy and still smelling like smoke if you got close enough to get a whiff.

"So you ready for the summer?" I ask nervously.

"Not sure, how about you?" she asked, smiling.

"Aaahh." Her skin was dark chocolate, smooth as warm butter and her voice was softer than Janet Jackson's. I stole a couple of glances and deposited them quickly into my memory bank. I turned from her almond eyes, praying to the heavens to let me be brave this one time. To give me the strength to ask her out. I begged, mentally hoping telepathy would reach God during rush hour, Por favor Jesu' Cristo look out for your boy one-time, but the metal doors slid open, and she got off. That was last week. Today, I got the holy ghost and an extra battery on my back.

Jerry Blood Knuckles was sexually active at eleven years old. I didn't even know what it was like to hold a girl's hand. "Boogie, if you go anotha' year without bustin' a nut, your balls are goin' to blow like an M-80 bomb on the fourth of July b'." Jerry Blood Knuckles said.

"Yo, I ain't no virgin man. I don't know what you talkin' 'bout b'." I lied.

"Yeah – yeah – yeah . . . name the last girl you smashed Boogie." He pressed.

"A gentleman never tells." As soon as the last word left my lips, Jerry Blood Knuckles busted out with a burst of laughter that could be heard bouncing all over St. Mary's walls.

Although I haven't seen Jerry Blood Knuckles in days, I kept hearing his laughter and thought to myself, "Nah yo, we can't be Suckah Sam for the fifteenth time. I gotta make my move on Becky Brown From The Boogie Down today'." This girl was the Mona Lisa of St. Mary's.

Next to the yellow Jerry Curl spray bottle, I put the afro pick back on the wooden shelves above the toilet. I flexed my muscles in the mirror attached to the medicine cabinet and thought boxing had great results. Undefeated, never lost a boxing match. When I got knocked down, I got back up. However, females broke a different type of fear into my heart. Getting rejected was more horrific than getting knocked out.

In middle school, I had small victories and created secret nicknames for myself in my bathroom. "You are the Macho Man Alex Savage, you're gone to ask that girl out, and she's going to say Yes Brother, Yes!" Sadly, I was better at boxing than getting girls. My coach used to say, "that girls will get ya killed faster than a glove will." I was willing to meet my execution with Becky Brown From The Boogie Down. I just was terrified of being rejected.

I threw on my damped Knicks shirt and cut-off black jean shorts. I open the bathroom door, walking towards the kitchen. You could hear my brothers fighting over the Mario Bros game in their bedroom through the hallway walls.

"I got next."

"No, it's my turn."

The eggs frying steaming with onions, tomatoes, and green bell peppers roamed through our three-bedroom apartment. The apartment's halls only allowed one person to walk through comfortably—with off-white walls covered with family pictures. I walked past our grey cockatiel, screaming for attention in a white cage next to a blue parakeet that seemed contemptuous in his smaller cage. My mom's on a corded phone talking with her sister cutting potatoes. The kitchen, like the hall, was a tight space, but everyone learned to keep their distance. Every room had barred metal windows except for the bathroom. There were eight of us living in this tiny apartment. Some slept on twin beds, others on floors, and my parents had their room. Every day the dishes piled up like a mountain shaped by forks, plates, burnt pots with white rice, and black beans seared to the bottom.

"Ale' laves los platos bien.", my mother says while holding the speaker part of the phone with her palm. "Yo sé que tienes prisa pero no te vas hasta que haces un trabajo bueno.", she complained.

"Wow, now you're acting like I can't wash dishes.", I said while not making eye contact so that she knew I wasn't protesting. My mother understood every word I said in English, although she did not speak one word. She lost the desire to learn English years ago. I took the steel wool and scrubbed the burned pot. The kitchen walls were a mustard color with dried oil stains on the ceiling, with a small fridge covered in Jesus and the Virgin Mary magnets. The wooden cabinets protested closing because they were jammed with dishes. Potted plants ran along the edges of our windows from the kitchen to the living room.

My mother used her potted plants for cooking, such as; oregano, rosemary, bay leaves. Other plants like yerba Buena and Aloe Vera were used for medicine. With all the windows open, you could hear the thousands of sounds coming into our thirteenth-floor apartment from the city. St. Mary's Projects is divided by train tracks that run through the city like arteries. The trains CLAK CLAK CLAK every two to five minutes with the conductor over the microphone saying, "Next Stop 3rd Avenue. Stand Clear For Closing Doors."

I cleaned the last dish.. My mother finished her phone conversation and asked me to throw the trash out. I sucked my teeth. "¿que tu piensas ?. . . tu no eres que mandas aquí.", she threatened.

"Mami, I'm just going to hang out with some friends downstairs. Por favor…" She didn't let me get another word in and told me to take the trash out. I cursed her name to the red trash chute next to two elevators right outside our apartment, in the public hallway. Mr. Gary came out of his apartment.

"Hey Alex, it's your summer break, right?" I remembered him being at least six feet tall with glasses, hair stubbles that covered some of the bumps on his face, light-skinned with a short fade cut. He seemed to be in his thirties or forties, living with his mother. Mr. Gary was one of the most generous people in St. Mary's projects. He was on his way downstairs when he said, "hold on, I got something for you and your brothers," and came back out with some candy. I don't remember what kind or what type of flavors, just a white bag filled with goodies. "So what do you have planned for the summer, young man?" He was highly confident. He held his head up high when he talked and looked you straight in your eyes without blinking. He was always smiling.

"I don't know, Mr. Gary, some basketball, maybe the public pool." I was lying just out of politeness. He pressed the elevator button and wanted to hold a conversation while he waited.

"Don't go wasting it. Every summer that comes is never the same as the last one. You'll be an old man before you know it." He was educated and extremely brave. He was the first openly gay man I knew in these projects, and that's asking for trouble. I wish I could be myself without having to impress anyone like Mr. Gary. I was thirteen trying to fit in. The peer pressure was stacking up. Yeah, everyone was used to seeing gays downtown in Manhattan, by the village, or by the fashion district, but not in St. Mary's. He talked to my mother like they were friends even though she spoke no English and he spoke no Spanish. She understood everything he said and would laugh hysterically, showing her nice pearly white teeth with one shiny gold crown. He was a gay happy man taking care of his mother. To me, you couldn't be any tougher than that. His family came first, and Mr. Gary lived by that code.

"Nah, I'mah just hang out with my friends," I told the truth, and his demeanor changed, and the energy shifted. I felt like I was supposed to say something profound, but the words did not produce themselves. Something like, "How are you so brave? What's it like being a family man? Do you ever get scared of being yourself? I want to be a nerd and read books, but my friends would kill." These words and ideas just swam in my head like lost baby pigeons. The elevator door slid open.

"Alright, be good now and tell your family I said hi." He didn't even look at me when he got in. I knew he questioned my friends because they teased him all the time, especially Jerry Blood Knuckles. He was the worst one.

As I opened the door to my apartment, I shook my head, trying to figure out how to tell my friends to take it easy on Mr. Gary. I knew Jerry Blood Knuckles would be difficult. The Ol' Heads were prepping him to be a street soldier. The Ol' Heads were constantly scouting for young recruits to deliver packages, transport guns, rob drug dealers, and war with neighboring projects. Middle school kids were easily impressionable with cars, money, and jewelry. In the early nineties, crack cocaine was king. Kids at fourteen were driving brand new Lexus cars without any license or driving experiences – buying them straight cash. Under the train tracks, you could hear them blasting Willie Colon or Eric B. and Rakim for five or six blocks down Westchester Avenue. Jerry Blood Knuckles was an up-and-coming new-age street super-soldier. He was chasing grown men down the street with bats. He was pistol-whipping drug dealers who were once considered kings in St. Mary's – who became junkies smoking their products. Jerry Blood Knuckles was moving in a different direction, and we weren't hanging out as much, but we were still a crew. We were still family.

My apartment was quiet whenever we started eating my mother's cooking. My mother made our favorite eggs, chopped baked potatoes, and Farina which looks like grits; the only difference is that it's sweeter. I was still thinking of Mr. Gary and felt maybe I should tell Jerry Blood Knuckles to give him a break. For now, Becky Brown From The Boogie Down was my mission.

Half the shootings that took place on our block during that time were from Jerry Blood Knuckles. Jerry Blood Knuckles, Danny Boy, B-Suave, Diesel, Scotty N' Tha Jets, Blue, Roc, Taz, Crazy Mike, Avery Ave, Corey Mr. Smooth, G-Man, Stevo, and Goyo we were all part of the same crew, the same family from St. Mary's. We became extremely close with every venture.

A month ago, Jerry Blood Knuckles dared me to ask Becky Brown Form The Boogie Down on a date. I was trying to impress him. I chickened out. I had no choice now, especially after I lied and told him I was not a virgin. I figured if I asked Becky Brown out on a date, then the pressure about my virginity would cease.

I walked past the yelling cockatiel when the shot echoed from our downstairs lobby, ringing through the elevator tunnel, bouncing off the hallway walls. I ducked instinctively out of habit, hoping that a stray bullet didn't enter our apartment. We were used to shootings in the summer, but this felt different. You could hear the people screaming and running from downstairs. I ran to my brother's room, shoes and clothes scattered everywhere. They were all staring out the window with my mother. The shot felt close. We could still feel the echo of the shot ringing throughout our building. There could've been another shot? Perhaps it was the fear that made the echo last longer than it did.

From my brother's window, we could see everybody running away from our building. My mother looked at me and said, "Tu no vas abajo te quedas aquí." She was correct; I needed to stay upstairs.

Things are quiet downstairs. There were still a small number of people crying from what the barred window allowed us to see. I went back towards the kitchen. I wanted to get my mind off of downstairs. The doorbell rang. My mother opened the door, and I ran right beside her.

"Ma'am have you seen this individual before?" Asked the Detective.

I knew that we could only entertain these guys for less than a minute. This is St. Mary's project, the walls have ears, and there are eyes you don't see watching you. Every floor held about eight apartments which meant about eight families were living in each of them. My building went up twenty-one stories, and that calculates into a lot of gossip. Anyone caught talking to the police might as well have their bags packed and ready to move before sunset. Your response can't be too quick or long because it will raise suspicion. You have to pretend to show interest, at the same time, give a body gesture suggesting you can't help. I took the picture from my mother, and he seemed taller in this Polaroid film. His face looked relaxed, and his caramel brown skin was smooth without a wrinkle. His eyes weren't glassy. "We have reasons to believe he's a suspect in a murder that happened . . ." I understood that Jerry Blood Knuckles, whose picture they were showing us, murdered my neighbor Mr. Gary. My mother's face filled with horror. She was shocked and could not respond to anything. Perhaps she remembered the moments she laughed with Mr. Gary or the many times she fed Jerry Blood Knuckles right in our living room.

"Sorry, officer, we can't help you," I said, my mother, stunned. I can feel her looking at me, and I avoid making eye contact with her. I closed the door, and my mother and I said nothing. St. Mary's Hip Hop Block Party canceled. My moment with Becky Brown does not happen and will never take place. This moment will leave a scar that will last a lifetime. My parents will forever see me in a different light.

The St. Mary's crew would suffer loss to drugs, alcohol, incarceration, indifference, internal disputes, and death. Some of us would remain connected, like B-Suave and I. Others would fade away, never to be heard from again. Several years from this moment, I will pass by Becky Brown without recognizing her at a bus stop. I will see

Jerry Blood Knuckles on 3rd avenue after serving his time as a minor. I will scream his name with nervous excitement, and we will both look at each other for less than a moment. From a few yards, I will be able to see that his knuckles will no longer be bloody or scabby. His stare will no longer be confident and full of rage. He will drop his head. He will turn his back to me and cross the street in the opposite direction. He will blend in among the busybodies pushing their way towards their destinations. A cold chill will blanket the surface of my skin as I come to the realization that the Jerry Blood Knuckles I knew died when he killed Mr. Gary.

Black Brown Boy

Elementary School
Black Brown Boy
use to beat cement walls
with   a closed fist
bom –bom - bom
whenever kids laughed at his poor English that is
      "Yo espoke con Luis"
            "Hahahaha", they joked, – "Yo espoke with Luis
that ain't no English you dummy . . .
                  It's I spoke with Luis
Hahahaha get back on that banana boat"
They ridiculed
made fun of him
laughed at him
but he would beat on them walls
Beat on them walls
Beat on them walls
bom – bom – bom
Black boy
Brown boy
Black Brown Boy
Beat that yellow wall and mumbled under his breath

Con che che concheko
Con che che con che
Bom bom
Con che che concheko
Con che che con che
Bom bom

Making Music
music and poetry was his therapy

and you can hear him down the halls of P.S. 5 elementary school
on beat

Che he concheko
Con che che con che
Bom bom x2

He told his peers how he wanted to be writer
"Ha Ha Ha Ha Ha" they laughed
How he wanted be a Poet
        "Ha Ha Ha Ha Ha" they laughed some more
An actor
Own a film company
Photographer
Publish books
Get an English degree
Be a teacher
        "Ha Ha Ha Ha Ha" they laughed even harder

But the Black Brown Boy
Kept beating them walls
Kept beating them walls
Kept beating them walls
Kept beating them walls

che che concheko
Con che che con che
Bom bom x2

He grew up in the Bronx
St. Mary's project
He was five then

when he moved there
he's been jumped
robbed
shot at
First shooting he witness he was 7 yrs old
mothers running crying pushing their babies' strollers
Rowdy Rod would push him down twenty flights of stairs
But he got up
Brushed himself off
Beating down them walls

Beating down them walls
Beating down them walls
With his fist

Che che concheko
Con che che con che
Bom bom x2

Making music
Writing poetry
You could hear him on the train
bus stops
down the avenue

Che che concheko
Con che che con che
Bom bom x2

Today
he's published eight books
owns his film and photography company
attended the Iowa's Writers Workshop

an MFA Graduate of Cal State
and this Black Brown Boy
Él está con nosotros en este momento
En serio
he is
I am the
Black Brown Boy
performing in front of you now
and the walls are gone

Che che concheko
Con che che con che
Bom bom x2

Don't Ever Stop Believing

Alex Avila
MFA CSUSB
AP

Exit Jackson Av
Westchester

Subway Map

Exit

Exit

POET T-SHIRT ON **SALE** AT AVILA PRODUCTION.COM

27

Avila Bucket Hat on sale at avilaproduction.com

Stay Strong Bottle